I Just Got a Letter from
Allyson Pringle

I Just Got a Letter from
Allyson Pringle

A novel by
Anya Bateman

DESERET
BOOK

Salt Lake City, Utah

This is a work of fiction Characters described in this book are the products of the author's imagination or are represented fictitiously.

Library of Congress Cataloging-in-Publication Data

Bateman, Anya.
  I just got a letter from Allyson Pringle / Anya Bateman.
      p.   cm.
  Summary: When Kendall Archer, Mormon straight-arrow, ends up becoming friends with the popular school clown, he discovers that she is a more complex person than pretends to be.
  ISBN 978-1-60641-028-8 (paperbound)
  1. Mormons—Juvenile fiction. [1. Mormons—Fiction.   2. Conduct of life—Fiction.   3. Interpersonal relations—Fiction.   4. High schools—Fiction. 5. Schools—Fiction.]   I. Title.
  PZ7.B29435Ial 2008
  [Fic]—dc22
                                                                    2008035744

Printed in the United States of America
Publishers Printing, Salt Lake City, UT

10   9   8   7   6   5   4   3   2   1

Acknowledgments

A big thank you to Lisa Mangum and Chris Schoebinger, who initially read this manuscript and believed in it. Thanks to Lisa as well for her encouragement and editing help with this and my previous book, and to Emily Watts, who took the editorial reins on this project.

Thanks as well to the many friends, neighbors, relatives, and ward members, "experts" in various fields, for answering my strange little questions such as "What's an item a wholesale electrical company would be shipping out?" or "What's a good science project?" Special thanks to my neighbor, Kristie Pitts, a busy teacher and a genuinely supportive friend, for once again providing me with the detailed information I needed in regards to high school schedules, class curriculum, and so forth.

And how would I have made it through this without the people I can always count on for completely honest input—my children? In spite of their own busy schedules with babies, callings, jobs, and everything, they always seem happy and willing to read and critique my writing projects. I am constantly amazed at their diverse and exceptional talents, which help me see things from many angles. Thanks especially to Les, our family's literary expert, who gave me some sound structural suggestions and who has a knack for seeing the whole picture when it comes to life as well.

Most of all, thanks to my ever-constant husband, Vaun, who, even though he's a go-to-bed-at-ten-and-get-up-at-six kind of guy, remains understanding and patient with my middle-of-the-night writing adventures and goes about his business of keeping our little boat afloat day in and day out without complaint.

Chapter One

So how'd your day go?" my buddy Arnold asked when he caught up with me the first day of our senior year. Static electricity was playing havoc with his peach-red hair again, strands shooting from his head like tiny laser beams. His clothes hadn't made it through the day in much better shape. My friend since third grade was kind of a dork by high school standards—but he was a cool dork in that he sincerely cared about others. Still does. He's on a mission in Australia right now caring about Australians.

"Oh, you know, your typical first day of school," I answered, lowering my trombone case so I could readjust my backpack. "My gym stuff's stuck in my locker, which for some reason doesn't want to open. Then I spent half of second period roaming the halls looking for room 211. You'd think after being at this school for two years I would know where they keep the rooms. But, umm," I grinned at this point and paused for effect because I had something to tell my friend that I knew could very well flip him into one of what you could call his *exuberance convulsions.*

"What?" Arnold lifted his narrow chin.

"Allyson Pringle's in two of my classes."

My friend's eyebrows shot up as his mouth dropped open. "You've got *Allyson Pringle* in two of your classes? Oh, man, you're one lucky bloke!"

Even back then Arnold peppered his language with Australian terms, when he couldn't have known he would one day be called on a mission to the land down under. One of those things you wonder about.

"Okay, how did you do that?" he continued. "How did you get two classes with the funniest and funnest girl in the whole school? You got connections or something? Wait—did Sister, I mean *Mrs.* Carru have anything to do with this?"

Arnold was referring to one of our school's assistant vice prin-cipals, whose real last name is Carruber with the accent on the *u*. Because she lived in our ward before she and her family moved to another ward in our stake, and even served as our Primary presi-dent, Arnold and I had a hard time remembering to address her as *Mrs.* and not *Sister.* Now that my brother and sisters and the Wanslot kids had graduated from Hollenda High School, Arnold, his sophomore twin sisters, Mrs. Carruber, and I were the only members of our Church who ambled through the halls of our mid-sized school on the outskirts of Kalamazoo, Michigan. The other high school age kids in the ward lived in the Central High boundaries.

"Of course Mrs. Carruber didn't have anything to do with it,"

I said, laughing a little at the thought. When it came to her job, Mrs. Carruber was proper beyond belief and did everything by the book. "Hey, all I can figure is I must just live right."

"I believe it!" Arnold was panting now, reminding me of my dog, Lucky Duck. But a dog can get away with panting at close range. At least Arnold didn't drool. "You gotta promise to tell me everything she says and does, and I mean *everything!*"

"I'll do my best," I said, trying not to sound as pumped as I was feeling. I wasn't about to let my feelings gush all over and out there like Arnold did.

"No, I mean it, Kendall," said Arnold. "Don't just try. You gotta do it! Remember every word that comes out of Allyson's mouth— everything she does. Maybe you should write it all down. I could use a good laugh too, you know. We can all use a good laugh!"

"When I take notes in Thorndike's, I think they'd better be history notes," I let my friend know. Having heard years before that Mr. Thorndike was the toughest teacher at Hollenda and maybe even in all of Michigan, I'd put off taking AP American History until my senior year because I wanted to make sure I had the study habits and experience required to make it in his class. Okay, yeah, I was being overly cautious as usual; I'd had good study habits since preschool. I probably would have done just fine if I'd taken history the year before. "Don't worry," I assured my friend. "I have the feeling it won't be much of a problem remembering what The Pringle says and does. Let's just hope she behaves herself in Thorndike's."

Arnold didn't look satisfied. "Man, I wish we could come up with one of those little recorders that the FBI and CIA use!" He stiffened his jaw and moved forward his teeth as if trying to come up with a source, but then he shook his head. "That's okay, you can just video her on a cell."

"Yeah, I'm sure teachers would love that, especially Thorndike." My friend was talking crazy now. Still, I was in such a good mood that I chuckled as I tapped at my right temple. "Don't worry, I'll record it all up here."

"A play-by-play?"

"A play-by-play!" I was feeling oddly important—as if I somehow really did deserve credit for Allyson being in my classes. Maybe it was Arnold bouncing around me like a Whac-A-Mole Gopher that was affecting my grip on reality.

Although Arnold's reaction was definitely up there at the hyperventilating level, it didn't surprise me. High interest and excitement were nothing new when it came to anything regarding Allyson Pringle. My buddy was only one of the hundreds at our school ravenous for updates on her jokes or antics. "Alysse," as she liked to refer to herself (pronounced like the classic *Alice in Wonderland*), was Hollenda's school clown—its jester—basically the top dog when it came to comedy. A professional comic couldn't have had a more devoted following. Bottom line, just as Arnold had said, she was funny. You honestly never knew what crazy thing she was going to do next. That was why in the halls, in between classes, we'd hear things like, "Did you see what Alysse wore to the game last night?" or, "Did you hear what The Pringle said in the cafeteria?" and so forth. Information would be happily exchanged. Then giggling and chuckling and even loud whoops would follow. I doubt there was a student at Hollenda who wouldn't have been eager to trade classes with me in order to spend those hundred or so minutes with Allyson Pringle every day. Having even one class with her could make not only your day but your semester and hey, as far as I was concerned, maybe even your life. Everybody clamored to be around this girl with the crooked smile and bright, mischievous eyes.

When I say *everybody* I should probably make it clear that I'm referring to the other students at Hollenda—her peers, in other words. When it came to teachers and adult personnel, it wasn't quite the same story. Even the normally easygoing Señor Alvarez, our Spanish teacher, hadn't seemed nearly as thrilled as the rest of us at having Allyson in his third period class. Not at first, anyway. Now that I look back and think about it, had I been a teacher, I don't imagine I would have been all that excited to find out I'd be dealing with the school clown all semester.

"Alysse and Alvarez have already butted heads over the seating arrangements," I told Arnold as we headed downstairs. "Alysse wanted to sit by Rhonda Pate and Dee Dee Smit." My mouth twitched and I glanced at Arnold out of the corner of my eye before I added the next part. "She was cool about it, but I don't think she was exactly overjoyed when Alvarez assigned her to sit next to *me*."

It took Arnold only a second or two to do the cartoonlike double take I was waiting for. His mouth popped open and he let out a "Whaaaaat! You're telling me you even sit by her?"

Chuckling happily as we reached the school's ground level, I stepped back to let him move ahead of me. "Just in Spanish—at least I will be, starting tomorrow." This time there was no hiding even my own excitement, and I could hear it in my voice. "Today she had to leave right after seats were assigned—some assembly practice or something. Then, in Thorndike's, she's across the room from me. But, yeah, in Spanish we'll be sitting next to each other." My excitement dimmed slightly at this point, however, because I was pretty sure I knew *why* Señor Alvarez had assigned Allyson to the seat next to me. He probably figured that if anyone in the class could have a subduing, maybe even dozing-off influence on her, it would be me. When I brought up this last part to Arnold, my voice lowered a few decibels.

"Hey, don't worry about *why* Alvarez put you next to her," said my ever-optimistic friend. "Just count your lucky stars she'll be sitting by you. You can be her straight man!" Arnold held the door open wide enough for me to slip through, then followed. "A comic can always use a straight man, right?" I knew he was talking about those old comedy duos where the more serious, sensible, and conservative sidekick lets his partner get all the laughs.

"If you say so," I muttered.

Chapter Two

One family home evening when I was around ten, Mom passed out three-by-five cards and had all of us write down the strengths we saw in each other. Thanks to Dad's insistence that we keep our comments positive, things went fairly well.

Kip got exciting descriptions such as *confident* and *good at sports*. Those are the ones I remember, anyway. My explosive brother, who's six years older than I am, was already looking really good on the basketball floor.

I'm sure my sisters each received their own impressive adjectives. I'm guessing we listed things like *friendly* or *talkative* for Lynette, the most socially savvy member of my family. Monica's list would have included things like *smart* and *athletic*. Monica was taking gymnastics at the time, but later on, when she grew too tall to be a gymnast, she took up volleyball. I'm guessing I wrote *kind* or *good friend* on her card. Monica is the closest to my age, and unless she was in a really insecure mood at the same time I was in teasing mode, we got along amazingly well.

I don't remember exactly what family members listed for me at that family home evening, but I can guess. They were likely adjectives I had heard even at that young age and probably considered boring: *responsible, conscientious, trustworthy*—things teachers had been putting in the comments section of my report cards since kindergarten.

Kip, just to give me a bad time, listed almost all of the thirteenth article of faith on his card to me: honest, true, chaste, benevolent, and so on. My brother always accused me of making him look bad, saying that my habit of getting to chores first thing even on Saturday mornings, for instance, was "sick."

"Get a life, man," he would yell as I vacuumed past his room. What he didn't realize was that doing what needed to be done when it needed to be done *was* my life. And it wasn't as if I didn't get recognition for that. Mom took me aside one day and said, "You know, Kendall, that I love all you kids, but someday you'll understand how nice it is to have a child you can completely rely on just to quietly go ahead and do good and right things even when nobody's looking over his shoulder." What could I do when she said things like that? I tried even harder.

"Maturity beyond his years" and "a serious approach to life," teachers had also written through the years on my report cards, and finally: "an amazingly honest boy."

It was Mrs. Farnsworth in fourth grade who wrote that last comment, and I know why she wrote it. During one of the spelling tests, I happened to glance over just as the girl who sat next to me lifted her paper, and I accidentally saw the word *pharmacy*. I ended up getting 100 percent on that test, but the fact that I'd seen that word really bothered me because even though I was *almost* completely, maybe even 99.9 percent sure I would have remembered how to spell *pharmacy* even if I hadn't seen it on my neighbor's paper, I wasn't 100 percent sure. I confessed this to Mrs. Farnsworth the next day.

"But you consistently get hundreds on your spelling tests," she argued. "You've gotten six hundreds in a row!" We were having a contest and she knew I was close to winning it. "But I'm not *positive*," I said.

When I entered the Porto Alegre North Mission in Brazil a few months after high school, I'd only been out two and a half months when President Phillips transferred me into the mission office to take care of the finances. He told me I struck him as someone who would have the patience and integrity to handle this detail-oriented job. Why I struck him like that, I'm not sure. Maybe the adjectives were stamped on my forehead by that time.

But we all have those lesser-known aspects or dimensions to our personalities as well. Nobody would have written *sensitive* on a card for my brother, for instance, but the guy sobbed his eyes out the summer after his high school graduation when Macey Hawkins dumped him for Ace Mackintosh (who was six years older and already had his own successful security systems business). I would never have guessed that my six-foot-five, macho brother could take anything so hard. Not that I blamed the guy for being upset. Macey was the first girl Kip had ever fallen for, and she *was* really cute. He freaked out when Dad said it was probably for the best. They'd had words over that. "Why do parents always say things like that?" he'd almost yelled. "It isn't for the best!" Well, as things turned out, Dad was right.

Without Macey to worry about, Kip ended up putting in his papers and going on a mission, which he maybe wouldn't have gotten around to if he'd remained joined at the hip with Macey and her friends. Once out there, my brother worked like a plow horse. It wasn't too long after he returned that he met my gem of a sister-in-law, Aubrey. To tell you the truth, I don't think he would have come anywhere close to being in her league if he hadn't grown so much during those two years, and I'm not talking about height. So things turn out. Aubrey can just look at Kip a certain way and he's up and doing chores. I've even seen him vacuuming. And his two little girls? My brother is cream cheese around them.

My sisters, too, both have those less obvious facets. Lynette, who's always been the family girly girl, once went after a bad guy who was pushing around an old neighbor lady. I'm guessing Lynette might have used the lamp base she was wielding if he hadn't been smart enough to make a run for it. I wondered if her husband, Josh, had seen that side of her before they got married.

And Monica, yes, good old Monica. Monica and her husband live in Ann Arbor with their twin baby boys. The sports girl is into nesting mode now and is always fixing up their little apartment and nursery. She's even into *cute*, something I never in my life thought I'd see. I miss her—miss them all. Sure, you wish you were an only child when all your siblings are around, stealing your food, getting in your face, picking on you. But then when they're gone you can hardly stand it. I was happy that I at least had Mom and Dad around during that last year of high school. But after observing them more closely, I realized that even parents have their dimensions. Dad isn't as "Mr. Business" and tough as he pretends. He has a gentle side, especially when it comes to my mother. And even though Mom's beyond neat and organized and generally very calm and in control, she tends to take on far more than one human being is capable of, then stresses out to the point of ranting at herself and even throwing things when she finds out that not even she can pull it off.

That leaves me. What I thought Arnold should have known, and what only my sister Monica was sensitive enough to write on the card she gave me at that family home evening (the only card I saved), is that although I'm basically serious about life, under the right circumstances and with the right people I can be fairly *funny*.

So it bothered me that first day of our senior year when Arnold suggested I be the straight man when I dealt with Allyson Pringle. What I really wanted to do was to joke around *with* Alysse and have some exchange—kind of a wit fest before or after class. I thought a longtime friend like him should know I was capable of that. Or was I? Well, we'd see. At last I was about to have that second chance I'd been hoping for.

Chapter Three

The first time I'd had the chance to talk with Allyson Pringle face-to-face hadn't been under the best of circumstances. The summer before my sophomore year, Dad helped me get a custodial job through a distant relative who worked for the school district. I honestly didn't mind doing that kind of work—cleaning toilets or even sweeping up strange debris. What did bother me was doing these things at Hollenda. I didn't complain often, but this time I did. "Dad, I really don't want to clean at my own school," I told him. "Practices have already started and really soon all the other kids will be right there in the halls. Isn't there something open at another school?"

I thought Dad would make some typical Pops comment such as *good hard work is nothing to be ashamed of, no matter where you do it*, but he surprised me. "I already asked about that," he let me know in a quiet voice, "and there's just nothing else available. Ed said that none of the other schools, even elementary, have an opening and that he felt lucky to get you this job at Hollenda. He promised to let us know if anything else opens up."

What could I do? Our family needed the money. The state economy wasn't in the best shape, and Dad's electrical supply business was struggling right along with it. It touched me that he had at least tried. Still, I can't say that I ever felt lucky to have that job, especially after the school year started. Monica had gotten into a fender bender right after she got her driver's license and wasn't allowed to drive for a while, and Mom couldn't very well pick us up right after school and then turn right around and take me back just an hour or two later. So every day after seventh period I studied in the school library until the halls were cleared. Then I rushed into the boiler room, slipped baggy overalls over my clothes, recorded the time on my time card, and, with lowered cap, swooshed that huge commercial broom through the halls with the speed of a brushfire.

If I moved fast enough, I found I could get out of the main part of the halls and the bathrooms by the time the practices were over and the clubs dismissed. Then, when students came back out into the halls, I hit the individual rooms. There were certain people I took extra trouble to avoid—several members of the football team, for instance. Ren Jensen, the six-foot-something junior varsity captain, had hairy legs and an even hairier attitude. All through junior high he and his friends had harassed me, constantly attempting to stick me in lockers or trash cans. It had started because I'd refused to turn over my science notebook to one of them. I knew if Ren or his friends saw me with that broom, I'd be toast.

13

That particular day, I'd gotten a late start because the football team had had a meeting before practice. It wasn't until after I thought everyone had finally cleared out that I started sweeping, and that was when I spotted Alysse at the end of the hall. Not that I knew it was her at first. She was walking normally for a change and wasn't pulling faces or doing anything absurd. In fact, she seemed to be studying something intently. I figured that this quiet, studious girl, whoever she was, would probably just pass by without even noticing me. It wasn't until she was within a dozen or so yards of me that I realized who she was.

Thanks to the cheer and drill tryouts and the opening assembly, Allyson had already established herself as somebody hysterically funny even by then. Now there I was, dressed in one of the costumes she would have worn as a joke or a spoof: oversized overalls, a too-large cap, holding a gigantic broom—only in my case it wasn't a joke.

I transferred the broom to my other hand and moved it behind me. Then, concerned that I looked like a merry-go-round horse with a pole coming out of my head, I pushed the broom to the side and leaned it against a locker. Next I tried to pretend I was opening that locker, a decision I quickly realized was silly and almost pitiful, especially when the broom started slipping.

Luckily, Alysse seemed oblivious to any of my scrambling. She continued studying what looked like a textbook as she headed straight toward me. When she got within about ten feet of me, I pulled myself up to my full height. Whether she liked it or not— and whether *I* liked it or not—I *was* cleaning the school and it was pretty stupid to pretend otherwise. But Alysse remained focused on her book and continued moving right at me. Was she kidding? I smiled hopefully at this point. I'd seen her play this trick on people. She would pretend she was about to run into someone, but then stop at the last second. Relaxing a little, I hoped that that was exactly what she was doing and that there was no way she could have gotten this close without noticing me. But my smile vanished as I realized that this wasn't a joke and that if I didn't move out of the way, she'd be plowing right into me. When I jerked back, my foot caught part of the broom base, and the broom handle once again flipped out of my hand, barely missing her.

Allyson pulled back in surprise. "Oh my gosh, where did you come from? I didn't think anyone else was down here." After I'd gotten control of the broom, our eyes met for the first time. Actually she'd looked *down* into my eyes, because I didn't get my growth spurt until my junior year.

"My fault," I said, trying to move the broom out of her path.

Now, at this point, Allyson could have snubbed me. She could have dismissed me as a nameless nobody—a pitiful squirt not even worth talking to—but she didn't do that.

"It was totally *my* fault," she said sincerely. "In fact, how are you doing? I mean, other than the fact that I just about knocked you over."

"Not bad," I squawked out, touched that she would even bother to ask. Clearing my throat, I glanced at her for a fraction of a second, looked back down, and tried once more. "I mean, I'm pretty good, thanks." And then I surprised us both by adding her nickname, "Alysse."

It was almost as if the sound of that name reminded Allyson of who she was or thought she was supposed to be, and she quickly moved into her comic persona. "Glad to hear that!" She started one of her routines with some kind of a fancy handshake. Hoping the broom was tucked safely between me and the biology lab room door, I followed along, all the while trying to think of something clever to say. Nothing came.

Ignoring my tongue paralysis, Alysse did a little twirl, curtsied, and said, "You take care now!" As she walked away, grinning over her shoulder and sashaying for my benefit and mine alone, I couldn't help myself, and I laughed.

It wasn't until a few minutes later, after I'd calmed down and was sweeping again, that I thought about the contrast between how she had approached—so serious and studious—and how she'd left. I guessed very few, if any, knew that Allyson was more than just a clown and that she, like the rest of us, had another facet or facets. I was pretty sure this more serious side wasn't something many knew about and suspected I was in on a secret. Soon I was whistling happily as I swept, partially because of this discovery, but also because, even though my tongue had failed me again, Allyson had treated me like I was somebody worth talking to.

For months after that event in the downstairs of Hollenda High—and I say "event" because, to a sophomore boy, having a girl as well liked and in the limelight as Allyson Pringle say hi to you *is* an event—I looked for Alysse every afternoon in hopes she would appear again at the end of that long hall. At night I practiced in our basement bathroom mirror what I would say should she ever show up again while I was working. I even brought some older jeans that were still semi-decent so I wouldn't be wearing the baggy overalls. But Allyson never did come down that downstairs hall again after school.

I did spot her often during school hours, in the front hall and so forth. But she was always busy with friends, talking, laughing, and, of course, *performing*.

By my junior year, I wasn't cleaning our school anymore. Dad had had to let a couple of his employees go, and I was helping him more at the warehouse. I'd given up hope of ever talking to Alysse face to face, anyway. I just joined the many others who watched her from a distance—your average fan. Unlike the others, however, I was watching for more than her antics and jokester moments. I was looking for hints of that other, more serious side of her that I had witnessed. And every once in a while, when she didn't think anyone was watching, I caught her quickly reviewing material or reading something or jotting down a note to herself, an earnest expression on her face. By the end of our junior year, I felt I knew Allyson Pringle a little better than most.

Now, at the beginning of my senior year, the prospect of finally having a second chance to make a better impression on Allyson had me practicing again. This year as I mouthed words into the mirror, somebody taller and more physically buff was looking back at me. I had changed so much that past summer that even my Aunt Betty hadn't recognized me when she stopped by after her European ballroom dance tour. But I'd grown up in even more significant ways as well. Just gaining experience through day-to-day living, such as the part-time bookkeeping I'd started doing for Dad's business (which included dealing with other businesses and even the IRS), and of course a lot of Church-related stuff, had helped me gain a little confidence. Okay, I had a ways to go, but I could see that, line upon line, I had made and was making progress. Being involved in the peer tutoring program and just reaching out to the people who seemed to need my help at our school had boomeranged and made me stronger and smarter as well. I'd figured out better what life was all about and didn't care quite as much what others thought. By my senior year, I was maybe still just as conscientious, but I wasn't the fearful and self-conscious little kid I'd once been.

But nobody's confident all the time, and that was why I was trying to come up with a clever way I could introduce myself to Alysse the following day. I have to say that in the past I'd succeeded in thinking up some pretty good one-liners there in our basement bathroom mirror. Down there, I was hilarious. But I was also well aware, thanks to past experience, that much of "funny" is in the presentation and that too often, planned-out funny doesn't hit the mark. I'd found out the hard way that it's generally a lot easier to be funny at home than in a real situation. Still, as usual, I felt the need to be completely prepared.

My dog grunted. "You're right, Lucky Duck, I worry too much. But have I told you I have two classes with Allyson Pringle and that I'm going to be sitting by her in Spanish? How's that, mutt? Huh?" When he realized I was talking to him, Lucky Duck let out a tiny woof and happily beat his tail on the throw rug. It doesn't take much to please a dog. I reached down to rub his ears, and then stood again to check myself. The slightly crooked tooth was still there, but at least last year's zits were pretty much cleared up and my face had filled out and was definitely looking better. I huffed out a sigh. Maybe I looked a little better than I had, but I still looked nothing like some of the GQ guys Allyson normally associated with. I lowered my eyebrows and leaned back, one eyebrow raised. "What's your line, Valentine?"

Negative. I made a gargling sound, shook my head, and lowered my eyelids. "Pretty pitiful, bloke," I said, adopting some of Arnold's Aussie slang. Okay, now I was definitely trying too hard.

Chapter Four

I should have known that no amount of planning or practice would be necessary because Alysse would beat me to the punch—or should I say punch *line*—anyway.

Within seconds after I sat down at my desk in third period Spanish, she extended her hand in my direction—at least, what I thought was her hand. It was actually a fake, Halloween-type hand—latex or rubber or something. It's a strange feeling to have somebody's hand pull right off, especially if it looks fairly real, which this hand did. "Aaah!" I jerked back, and in the process, the hand flipped into the aisle. I laughed nervously, staring at it.

Allyson's gesture definitely broke the ice. "Good ta meetcha, honey," she drawled in the hillbilly accent she'd often used since our sophomore year's school play, *Li'l Abner*. Batting her eyelashes, she added, "Sorry if I skeered ya."

"Good to meet *you*," I said, still a little flustered, but also flattered at having been the butt of Allyson's joke.

"She found another victim, huh?" Carlin Stevens said. One of our school's senators, Carlin, who sat a few seats closer to the front, had never spoken to me before. "She got me with that last year. Hey, Pringle," he said, switching to Alysse. "You gotta come up with some new material." Grinning, he reached down to pick up the hand and flung it back to her.

I looked around me, fully aware that I'd just been had, but not terribly upset about it. I definitely hadn't had the first word, but at least Alysse and I were already interacting. Then I surprised myself with an on-the-spot comeback. "Hey, thanks for giving me a hand there."

Allyson lifted her chin and raised her eyebrows and one corner of her full mouth. "Pretty clever, Mr. Archer."

I flushed at the compliment and the sound of my last name coming from Allyson Pringle's lips. If she noticed I was nervous, she was kind enough not to let on. In fact, she spoke out of the corner of her mouth then. "I'll bet you ten dollars Alvarez has no clue you know how to joke around." Without taking her eyes from me, she reached into her Minnie Mouse book bag and pulled out a couple of pencils, a pen with a huge orange feather attached, and a Betty Boop notebook. I expected her to say something more and she did. "You do realize he probably wouldn't have put me next to you, if he'd known? It's obvious he's on a major discipline streak—you know, the first week of school gotta-be-tough syndrome." Allyson raised and lowered her eyebrows twice, something I'd seen her do many times before, just never from right across the aisle.

"I'm guessing you may be right about that," I heard myself agree.

"And I'm guessing that teachers probably believe you're . . . umm . . ."

I lifted my hand to prevent her from continuing. "I know. I know."

"Uh-huh, uh-huh . . . so this isn't the first time, right? I'll bet the troublemakers get put by you all the time. It's that old trick teachers pull out of their bag. Stick the troublemaker next to the straight arrow."

"Hey, I wouldn't call you a troublemaker," I said. Then I heard myself add, "But you *are* pretty entertaining." My face warmed a little at the word *pretty* and I hoped she wouldn't think it was a Freudian slip—because Allyson *was* pretty. Behind the quirky glasses, her eyes were bright and alive even when she wasn't up to something, and up close her dark, chin-length hair glistened with some lighter highlights you didn't notice from far away.

"Oh, so what you're saying is that I'm a little *too* entertaining? Is that what you're saying?" she asked, unfazed.

"Okay, sometimes, yeah, you're a little too entertaining," I conceded, nodding.

Allyson again seemed to like that. "An Honest-Abe type, huh?" Grinning now, she smacked my hand with her real live hand, which was just smaller than mine. "Well, you know what? I think we're going to get along just fine, umm . . . Alfredo, is it? No, um . . ." We'd been assigned Spanish names the day before and Señor Alvarez had asked us to start using them. "Now, what's your Spanish name again?"

"Armando."

"Oh, yeah. Well, Kendall-Armando, you know what I predict? I predict we're going to get along fantastamously." She tried to get me to do some hard-to-follow handshake thing then (just as she had done two years before in the hall when I was a sophomore), and I was happily trying to follow along once more, when I noticed that Señor Alvarez had come in, was ready to begin, and was watching Alysse and me with a concerned, *Have-I-just-made-a-big-mistake-putting-those-two-together?* expression. The smile sluffed off my face as I sat up straighter in my seat, moved back my shoulders, and cleared my throat. That automatic response seemed to reassure Señor Alvarez that I wasn't planning on causing any problems in his classroom. His face relaxed, but then he seemed to remember his intent to make a tough impression and he furrowed his brows once again. But when Allyson complimented him in Spanish on his bright red-and-yellow tie—or attempted to, anyway—he had some trouble hiding his amusement.

Señor Alvarez wasn't what I would call the world's greatest actor. Neither am I. I wondered if it was obvious—and I was afraid it was—how thrilled I was feeling that Alysse and I had already interacted and that it had gone really well. This time I hadn't choked and I hadn't panicked. Maybe earlier I had wondered if all the confidence I'd gained in the past year or two was about to evaporate, but once I'd had the chance to visit with Alysse a little more, it had all worked out. Just like she'd said, it looked like we were going to get along *fantastamously.*

During lunch, I had to force myself several times to stop grinning. But I couldn't help letting it out a few hours later when

Arnold rushed me at my locker, eager for a report on how my first time sitting right next to the comedy star of the school had gone. My grin reemerged, causing Arnold to begin panting anxiously again, his mouth wide. "So she was there today? She was in class?"

"Oh yeah, she was there."

"And you talked to her?"

"We talked in third period."

"And?"

"We got along really well."

"Yeah?" Arnold nodded wildly. "So come on, come on, tell me more. Tell me everything!"

Arnold really could be such a dweeb, but I honestly didn't mind at that moment. I was more than glad to report what had happened in Alvarez's. Soon I was sounding like my sister Lynette back in the days when she shared far too many details with her best friends.

Arnold encouraged me by slurping it all up like a giant syringe. At one point he let out a loud war whoop: "Ha! A fake hand? A fake hand! I tell you, only Allyson Pringle would come up with something like that."

"You're right—only Alysse gets away with stuff like that," I said, looking around with concern. Lexie Baxter, who had a locker next to mine, was leaning in our direction.

"So whad'ya say, whad'ya do?" asked Arnold.

I lowered my voice and told him my response, glad he had asked, but wondering how much Lexie was hearing. Plenty, it seemed. "You have a class with Allyson Pringle?" she asked anxiously, allowing her front teeth to experience daylight for a change.

"Two classes," I answered, my chest swelling in self-importance once again.

"Oh, wow! Lucky!" Lexie lifted her hand and I slapped it.

"Alysse shook his hand with a fake hand," Arnold told her. "Kendall here freaked."

After they'd both finished hooting, Arnold repeated to me, "Okay, now this is exactly the kind of stuff I was talking about. Every day I hope you'll give me this kind of a full report with details. I mean, I need a good laugh as much as you. Memorize it like you'll be memorizing material for your physics tests."

"Me too," said Lexie, sniffing and moving closer. "I wanna hear too."

"Yeah, tell all of us," bellowed Bernard, a mop-haired junior friend of Lexie's who'd suddenly bounded into the picture as well.

"Fine, I will. I will." I said staring at them in amazement. *Yup, Allyson had a following.*

Chapter Five

I didn't need to report to Arnold or anyone else what Allyson did the next day. By the time I saw Arnold, just about everybody in the school had already heard that she had come into history class wearing the oversized Dutch boy outfit she'd worn in the "Welcome to Hollenda High" assembly earlier in the day.

"Sorry to be dressed like this, but somebody stole my regular clothes," she explained to Mr. Thorndike before he had a chance to rail on her.

"Oh, I see," he replied in a sarcastic manner, his eyes narrowed, his chin thrust forward.

"Really, I'm not kidding. If I were doing this just to be a troublemaker I would have worn the wooden shoes and the round hat. But you can see I just stuck to the basic pants and shirt," she continued.

As a few of the bolder kids snickered, I pressed my back against my seat with concern for my new friend. Maybe you could get away with going on like that with some teachers, but she had to know you couldn't do it with Thorndike. Besides, the clothes were anything but basic. The pants were huge and puffy, and the doubled-breasted shirt-jacket thing, even without the shoulder pads, was gigantic. Although it was obvious she'd removed most of the stuffing, the enormous shoulder inserts were still attached, and the rest of the shirt hung down her arms. Danny Karlowski finally laughed outright, but even he didn't dare really let it out like he would have in any other class. Next to him, Bret Nuswander, an off and on buddy of Ren Jensen's, grinned arrogantly and let out a snort or two as well, but then even he pulled back slightly in his seat, his eyes on Thorndike. Molly Engright, who'd been in my geometry class the year before, shook in quiet laughter, her lips puckered together. His face as tight as the drum he played in orchestra, Jake Huong's chest was vibrating.

I glanced at Mr. Thorndike, then looked back at Alysse. There'd been something in her eyes and the tone of her voice that made me feel she was telling the truth—that her clothes really had been taken. It didn't seem all that far-fetched that someone would pull that kind of prank on her, possibly a get-even-but-all-in-fun kind of stunt. My bigger concern was how Thorndike was going to react to all this. I could tell by the way her head was slightly tilted that Alysse might be worried about that herself.

It was obvious by his expression that Thorndike, along with just about everyone else in the classroom, believed that Alysse had worn the Dutch boy costume just for effect. His mouth twitching, he attempted to flip his pen into his shirt pocket, but, possibly because his hand was shaking, he missed the opening several times. Only after three attempts, and a stop to check exactly where the pocket was, did he finally hit the mark. "I'm going to excuse you immediately to go change back into your regular school clothes, Miss Pringle," he said, his teeth bared. "This is unacceptable attire and I think you know that."

"Well, then, I'll have to go home because somebody really did steal my clothes." Allyson was lifting her hand, palm side up, her voice a half octave or so higher than usual. Again I sensed her concern, which the other kids in the class —at least the ones who were still grinning into their textbooks—didn't seem to be picking up on.

"So be it, young lady," said Mr. Thorndike in a voice so cold it could have frozen lava.

"Okay, but . . ."

"And *now* would be an excellent time," he continued.

"Fine, I'll leave, then." Allyson gathered up her things and rose, alarming me even more by continuing to make comments. "The shirt was one of my favorites, too," she muttered. "The jeans weren't the best, but it was a really good shirt. If anyone finds out who took my clothes, tell them I really want that shirt back. At least they didn't take my shoes." Again I got the impression she wasn't kidding. But did she need to keep talking about it?

Once again, Mr. Thorndike wasn't about to let that go. "Miss Pringle, did I somehow give you the false impression that it was all right for you to continue disrupting this class?"

"No, sir, you didn't, but—"

"Then I suggest you say nothing further and exit this room immediately if not sooner, so that the rest of us can begin the history lesson for today." He spoke slowly, spacing the words, enunciating them with venom. "That is, I believe, why we come here daily—to study history. And so far we've wasted approximately," he looked at his watch, "seven minutes of time we already don't have enough of, simply because you made the choice to wear inappropriate clothing to class. Now, if this were a comedy club, maybe that would be acceptable, Miss Pringle, but we're not here for a comedy performance." He looked around. "Are we, class?"

A few barely audible no's were mumbled.

"What was that? Mr. Mallow, Miss Fern?"

The no's were clearer now.

"I understand that, sir," Alysse continued, "but like I said—"

"Miss Pringle!" He was almost shouting. "Leave now!"

"Yes, Mr. Thorndike, sir!" I was half afraid Alysse would click her heels together and salute. Instead she pulled the wide pant legs around the corner to the back and continued moving down the aisle.

My seat in Thorndike's class was in the second row from the back and there was an empty seat behind me. As Allyson passed along the back of the room she muttered just loudly enough for those of us near the back to hear: "It could have been worse. I was a windmill in the assembly last year."

Okay, now she *was* being funny on purpose, and I tried my hardest to keep my mouth from quivering, but couldn't help myself. I was mortified when a small snort escaped. Mr. Thorndike flipped his head in my direction. When he saw my concern and embarrassment, however, he bypassed the reprimand and just raised an eyebrow instead. Still, like a bull pawing at the ground, he needed someplace to direct his ire, and he narrowed his eyes at Danny Karlowski, who had laughed earlier *without* remorse afterward. But it was obvious that it was Allyson he was the most livid with. He turned back to her, his small eyes following this girl who'd had the audacity to joke in his classroom until she finally exited. "Maybe now we can get something accomplished!" he snapped.

Jen Fern, whose timing was often off, wasn't able to conceal a delayed giggle completely, and Mr. Thorndike paused for a few seconds, moved his eyes slowly in her direction, and glared at her over his glasses. Jen pulled back her shoulders and looked down at her desk, her full face flushed. A look from Thorndike could pierce you to the bone marrow.

"I'm seeing several potential problems developing in this class that I would highly suggest we correct immediately," he said as he continued staring down unlucky Jen. Then he scanned the room, stopping at the regulars, the guys in the back and Danny, but also Jake and Molly, and then, to my surprise, at me.

Being distrusted by a teacher felt strange because it so rarely happened to me. In fact, it was almost laughable that any teacher would think I was a problem.

After a few minutes, Thorndike seemed to calm down somewhat, but when Alysse reentered his classroom ten or fifteen minutes later, his eyes bulged over his glasses. "I believe I sent you to the office!"

"I told Mrs. Carruber you wouldn't like this, but she sent me back here anyway because she didn't know what to do with me," Alysse said as she moved toward his desk. "She gave me this note."

There was no arrogance in her tone, and she didn't so much as blink at those in the room snickering. In fact, Alysse, possibly with Mrs. Carruber's help, had pinned back the Dutch boy pants to ease away some of the fullness. Nevertheless, Mr. Thorndike's face tightened even more, and his eyes narrowed once again as he surveyed the note. "Very well, be seated, please!" Smoke might as well have been billowing out of the top of his head. "I'll have a little visit with Mrs. Carruber about this after class."

Now I even worried for Mrs. Carruber. But it was Alysse I was most worried about. We were barely into the semester and she was already on super lousy terms with the one teacher you really didn't want to be on lousy terms with.

Chapter Six

Even though I honestly didn't think Alysse had worn the Dutch boy outfit to history just for laughs, I totally got why everybody else thought she had. I mentioned earlier that she was big on costumes. Clowns are like that. Allyson had showed up for both cheer and drill tryouts in her father's old army fatigues, for instance.

Drill team members were chosen by adult judges, but had it been up to the students, Alysse would have made the team without any problem. When it came to the cheerleaders, the students did vote, but still the judges' opinions counted 25 percent, and the adviser and her assistant had the final word. In other words, even though it appeared as if we were choosing, adults were actually making the final decision. Even at that, and considering the fact that it had all been a joke anyway because she had no gymnastic skills whatsoever, Alysse had barely lost. The next year, however, our junior year, when she ran for student body vice president (dressed this time in an oversized business suit and gigantic bow tie) and used portions of all the finalists' talks for her own, she won by a landslide.

The fact that she hadn't made either cheer or the drill team didn't stop Allyson from joining the teams anyway. While the cheerleaders did their flips and toe touches at the game sidelines, Alysse would hurry over to wave at the crowd and do a crooked cartwheel or a lopsided somersault or two, then raise both arms high. The students in the bleachers would stand on their toes and jump on one another's backs to see her. For obvious reasons, the cheer adviser didn't like it much when Allyson joined her squad uninvited. In fact, word got around that the teacher had complained to the second assistant principal that Alysse made her squad look bad. But the cheerleaders themselves never seemed to mind and would applaud and laugh at Alysse and with her. What else *could* they do when Alysse got more response than they did in their attempts to get the crowd charged up? And it wasn't as if she barged in during their competitions or halftime performances. She knew when to butt out.

Those of us in the stands loved the girl for being so willing to make a fool of herself and illustrate just how really bad a normal person can look doing cheer. Maybe it was because, like Alysse, most of us couldn't come anywhere close to doing a flip or back handspring, not to mention a decent cartwheel. Maybe seeing how awkward Allyson was willing to look made the rest of us feel better about ourselves.

In an effort to be a good sport, the drill team adviser invited Allyson to perform with the team in their at-home halftime novelty number. We held our sides laughing when Alysse came out as one of the giant marshmallows, and we all knew within seconds which marshmallow she was. The team got a standing ovation for that performance. Or, I should say, *Allyson* got a standing ovation.

Alysse was in her best form, however, when she performed in our school plays. In *Li'l Abner* she brought down the house as tough, old, weather-beaten Granny. "Doggone it," she'd said ever since.

The next year, when we put on *The Music Man*, Mrs. Dallask, the drama teacher (one of the few adults in Allyson's fan club) begged Allyson to consider the part of Marian, the librarian. But Alysse chose to play Eulalie Shinn, the pompous mayor's wife. "I'm more of a character actress," she claimed.

I went to the musical that year for the same reason almost everyone else did: to see Alysse in the Grecian urn dance. Nobody left disappointed. Not only did she ham it up to the max, but she inspired the school's star dancers to immerse themselves in the role of middle-aged, uptight matrons with such enthusiasm that I laughed till I cried. We all did.

Even with all that, the incident in Mr. Thorndike's class would, I'm guessing, have toned down even the most costume-loving of clowns, but not Alysse. Oh, no. That very next Friday, at the first football game of our senior year, she was at it again. Allyson had talked some of her girlfriends into putting on oversized football jerseys and giant helmets, and they welcomed the team by running out onto the field with them.

Arnold had had to come early to help the band set up, and I'd taken Abe Stanley, someone I knew from Little League baseball days, up on his offer to drive me and a few others to the game. Next thing we knew, Alysse and her friends were tossing a two-foot stuffed football back and forth out on the field.

"Go, Alysse!" I shouted. Then, with a happy chortle, I looked around proudly at the cheering students who were once again climbing over each other to get a better look at what Alysse and the rest were up to. Even our official school mascot stood there flat-footed in his wooden shoes laughing in Allyson's direction. When Alysse somehow managed to kick the huge ball between the posts, the fans and the players on both teams erupted into cheers. "She's crazy," I kept saying to Abe as I laughed along with everybody else.

I wondered that night—and I've wondered since—how she got away with what she did: the marshmallow solos, the impromptu cheerleading stunts, things no one else would dare do. Me, for instance. I would no more have dared to run out onto a football field in funny clothes than fly to Havana for lunch. I think that afternoon I decided that we were in completely different spheres, Allyson Pringle and I. That's why I never in the world would have guessed that we would continue to get along as well as we did.

Chapter Seven

Unlike Thorndike, Señor Alvarez, just as Alysse had predicted, shed his gotta-be-tough image within days. Our Spanish teacher was proving to be a kick, and he let us know by his responses that as long as things didn't get completely out of control, he didn't mind having a good time with us. I have to say he was cool enough to help us recognize where to draw the line, however, and we cooperated by staying pretty much within reasonable boundaries.

It didn't take Señor Alvarez long at all to plug into our class's dynamics, and he soon began taking Allyson's antics in stride. I imagine the man realized he was never going to get this free spirit to comply completely with class rules. Sure, he probably would have preferred that she tone it down more, but I think he could see that if the class was going to get anything done, he would need to work with this girl. Go with the flow, as they say. So that was what he did. As long as Alysse didn't get completely carried away, he seemed to be okay with her behavior and even interacted with a punch line of his own once in a while.

What can I say? You had to like his style. I'm guessing the fact that Alysse seemed to pick up Spanish quickly, got her assignments in, and did well on tests could have had a little to do with his attitude toward her as well. Not that her good grades were something she flaunted. It didn't surprise me that she did her best to underrate herself in that department. When Señor Alvarez complimented her on an A on our first full test, she had a ready explanation: "I think there's a toreador somewhere back in my bloodline whose genes pop up now and then."

"I see," said Alvarez. "Just don't start fanning a red cape around and shouting *Olé*."

We got a kick out of that. And because of those few feet of extra rope Alvarez willingly extended, I discovered one day toward the end of September that I wasn't nearly as anonymous at Hollenda High as I'd thought.

I was up at the chalkboard, playing a game we had nicknamed the Spanish Inquisition. I absentmindedly chewed on the chalk for a second or two as I concentrated. Quick as a cat, Alysse called out, "Kendall Archer, what are you doing? Get that chalk out of your mouth! My gosh, it looks like you're *smoking!*"

"Señor Alvarez," she said then, turning in our teacher's direction, "how do you say *no smoking* in Spanish? Kendall-Wendall—I mean *Armando*, here—is not allowed to be smoking!"

"*No fumar*," Alvarez responded with a patient smile.

"And how do you say *word to the wise* in Spanish?" asked Alysse.

Word to the wise? I tilted my head.

When Alvarez hesitated, Alysse proclaimed: "It's the Mormon health code!"

Stunned by the comment, I pulled the chalk from my lips and didn't close my mouth for several seconds.

"Uh-oh, let's not go there," said Señor Alvarez, glancing at me with concern. Alvarez was no doubt wondering exactly where Allyson was heading with her comments; he looked like he might have been fearful that she'd said too much already. There was protocol regarding people's beliefs. But what I didn't notice on his face was *surprise.* Señor Alvarez was reacting as if he, like Alysse, already knew I was a Latter-day Saint. In fact, as I walked back to my seat, it struck me that not a single person in that classroom was acting as if my being a Mormon was any big news. Dennis Craig, for instance, quickly returned to the vocab cards he'd painstakingly made for himself. Dee Dee had chuckled, but now she had pulled out her lip gloss and was applying it nonchalantly. Carlin lifted one corner of his mouth as he stretched out his arm and expanded his fingers. I had the distinct feeling that Alysse hadn't let any kind of cat out of any kind of bag with her proclamation. People in my Spanish class were acting as if they already knew.

But how? I couldn't figure it out. *I'd* never said much to anyone about my religion. I'm sorry to say that I wasn't exactly your enthusiastic member missionary. I blamed it on basic shyness. Although it was true that I interacted pretty well now, it takes some extra metal in the spine to really get out there and take advantage of missionary opportunities. Oh, there were a few people I'd mentioned things to, here and there. When my biology lab partner the year before had told me she planned to smoke pot with her cousin during the Christmas break, I'd lectured her to the moon and back. But it wasn't as if I'd quoted scriptures to her or something. Then, when I was asked to play my trombone at our ward's Christmas party, I invited a couple of other orchestra members to participate with me, but they hadn't even stayed for refreshments. I also remember saying something about family home evenings to a sophomore I had tutored a few times during my junior year.

I'm guessing the guys I ate lunch with knew because we'd all had lunch together the year before as well, back when Arnold had the same lunch. But that was seriously about it. I wondered if this had anything to do with my brother and sisters. Yet Kip, Hollenda basketball hero though he was, hadn't set foot in the school for years, and Lynette, though she was popular with people who knew her, wasn't that well known throughout the school. Monica, who'd grown to be six feet by ninth grade, had kept her head down for the most part except when she was playing volleyball. Were Arnold and his sisters spreading the word?

As Allyson watched me return to my seat, she studied my face, a slightly sheepish expression on her own. I could tell she was wondering if maybe she *had* stepped over some invisible line by mentioning the Word of Wisdom.

I decided to keep her guessing. My face void of any expression, I opened my Spanish textbook and didn't take my eyes from it. But then I faked a cough.

Alysse's head popped up like a bedspring and I could tell she was grinning in my direction. I coughed again. "I really do need to quit smoking the chalk," I quipped, just loud enough for her to hear.

"Ha!" Allyson whipped around to Lakeesha Campbell. "So did you hear that? Kendall here only likes to make people think he's super serious, but you just heard that, right?"

"Hey, all I did was cough," I said with mock innocence. "Can't a guy cough?"

"Uh-huh, *chalker's* cough," she said with a wide grin. "I tell you," Alysse continued to Lakeesha, "you've gotta watch this guy."

Lakeesha chuckled uncertainly and Daphne Price leaned around to take a second look at me as well. Even Rhonda, two rows away, turned in our direction to see what was going on.

"What's Allyson talking about?" I said, my mouth twitching as I lowered my head and started working on the vocabulary questions.

"See, there he goes again," Alysse said.

After Lakeesha lost interest and turned to see what James Domrose was up to, I smirked at Alysse ever so slightly. Alysse whipped around again. "Okay," she said. "Did you see that look on his face? Shoot, you missed it again." Then, noticing that Señor Alvarez had stood and was giving us the "You're taking advantage of my good nature" look, Allyson called out, "*Lo siento*, Señor Alvarez," and lifted her fingers in a V.

Señor Alvarez shook his head and sighed good-naturedly. "*Tranquilo.*"

But Alysse, obviously intrigued, kept darting glances at me throughout the class period, an amused expression on her face. By conversation time, she had apparently figured out I had a question. "*¿Qué pasa?*" she asked. "You've got an eyebrow thing going on."

"*Nada. . . .*" I laughed, "except maybe . . ."

"What?"

I went ahead and said it. "I guess I was just wondering how you knew what church I belonged to and why nobody else in the class seemed surprised either."

"Uh-oh, was it supposed to be a secret?"

"Oh no." *Hardly,* I thought. "It's just that I didn't think all that many people knew, that's all."

"Hey, everybody knows when you're different," Alysse stated matter-of-factly. "It's just the way it works. And you'll have to admit that you're definitely not your average, run-of the mill, foul-mouthed, flagrantly truant student."

"There are quite a few others who aren't flagrantly . . . well, what you just said. *You're* not, and nobody thinks *you're* Mormon."

"That's because I'm *not* Mormon."

"Okay, I'll have to think about that one."

"You do that," she grinned, tapping me on the hand with the feather end of her pen.

"*Isabela y Armando—Español, por favor,*" Señor Alvarez reminded us.

"*Sí, Señor,*" said Alysse, responding to her Spanish name. "*¡Pronto!*"

"*Sí, Señor,*" I repeated, automatically complying or at least looking like I was. In truth I was still thinking about what Alysse had just said and having a hard time accepting it. Was I really all that different?

41

I looked over at James Domrose, who was flexing the scorpion on his bicep, and then at another guy sitting on the next row, who'd stuffed something in his mouth that I was guessing wasn't gum, his orange salamander earring dancing with each chew. Okay, maybe I *was* different. I'd just had no idea anybody had been noticing.

Once again Alysse seemed to know what I was thinking. "There's nothing wrong with your kind of different, believe me," she said quietly as Alvarez hurried to the supply closet to get some vocab quizzes. "In fact, you remind me of my brother, Pete. No offense, but he's a little over-the-top conservative, just like you. Like he's forever warning me to tone down and be careful. *Moi?* Even now that he lives back east he's calling me all the time to check up on me. Pete got accepted to Yale." I heard a lilt of pride in her voice.

I appreciated Allyson's attempt to comfort me, but again, I sort of doubted her brother was LDS.

Still curious, during lunch I asked Parry Lunder, who'd joined us at our table for the first time, if he knew what religion I was. Lunder and I had never had any classes together, and our Hollenda paths just hadn't crossed, for some reason—not even once. I didn't know anything about *his* religion or personal beliefs.

"Sure," Parry said, flipping open his sub sandwich and picking off the onions. "You're Mormon."

Chapter Eight

Things were crazy at our house. My sister Monica had called us from Utah a week or so into her semester at Utah Valley University to let us know that she and Rulon, her roommate's brother, were in love and wanted to get married at the Christmas break.

My mother had been whirring away on her old Singer in the computer/sewing room ever since, her face openly smiling one second, pinched the next. At the same time, Dad had been working overtime on the computer, trying to generate some additional sales to help pay for extra wedding expenses.

Generally my parents close up shop after family prayer, but that night they were still working close to midnight. Mom wasn't actually using the machine anymore, just cutting out or something, but I could hear her and Dad quietly discussing wedding plans, finances, and so forth. I don't think they realized how sound carried down that hall; even though I heard only an occasional word clearly, the low drone kept me awake. Then again, maybe I stayed awake because I was worrying along with them about how as a family we were going to pull this wedding off on such short notice. I happened to know that we weren't exactly wallowing in the extra funds.

Anyway, I was so tired that next day in homeroom English (not to mention early morning seminary) that I wasn't really paying attention to the announcements on the interschool channel. When I heard Allyson's name, however, my eyes popped open. "What was that?" I asked the guy who sat next to me. "What'd they just say about Alysse?"

"She's in the finals for homecoming queen," he replied, his upper lip curled up in amusement.

"No lie?" I chuckled happily.

I wasn't the only one laughing. "Good for Alysse!" Fantasia Farnell crooned.

"Yeah, good for The Pringle!" laughed the guy next to her.

April McKuen, who'd been nominated for some princess or queen the year before, shook her blonde curls and said, "She is so not the type." But then even she couldn't help smiling.

"I'd say it's good she's not the type," Janette Osborne chipped in. "Only let's just hope she doesn't show up as a Viking again, like she did at the dance last year."

That got several more laughing.

A few minutes later, while our teacher, Mrs. Cavanaugh, a reserve naval officer, was sharing with us in a booming voice the difference between metaphors and similes, I tried to come up with a clever way to congratulate Alysse. After class I thumbed through my Spanish dictionary, hoping I could find out how to say it in Spanish. I thought Alysse would get a kick out of that.

"*Felicidades,*" I practiced under my breath a couple of times during second period and once or twice down the hall to third period Spanish.

But I didn't get it out of my mouth.

"You!" Alysse boomed out the second I walked in the Spanish room door. She was pointing at me. "I need YOU in my home-coming skit!"

Before I had a chance to respond or even react, Allyson lowered herself into her seat next to me. "Here's the scoop. We're doing a cowboy scene. You know, singing, dancing—you love that kind of stuff, right? A real showman."

That lifted a few heads.

"Let's just say that I sing and dance about as well as you cheer," I responded.

"Ha, he got you on that one, Alysse," said Daphne, sticking a piece of gum into her wide and grinning mouth.

"Then you must be an amazing singer and dancer!" Alysse said. "Because everybody knows what a phenomenal gymnast I am." That made people around us snicker, even Dennis Craig, who let out kind of a wheezing sound. Carlin smiled but turned forward.

Since Señor Alvarez was up front now and practically doing gymnastics himself trying to get our attention, I turned to face forward too, excited and, yeah, flattered that Alysse wanted to include me in her skit. But it was one thing to make a few cracks in a classroom setting and far and away another thing to sing and dance on a stage in front of the whole school. There was no way I felt ready for something like that.

After class, I was glad to see Alysse busy recruiting some others among the more real showmen of the school, including Tallulah Barlow and Tyrone Brown. Tyrone immediately adopted a western stance, his thumbs in his pockets, his head cocked back. Parker Teal hurried over as well. It didn't look like Alysse would be having any trouble rounding up "cowpokes"; she wouldn't be needing me. But the girl I already considered a friend apparently didn't agree. I was almost halfway down the hall when I heard my name. I knew the sound of her voice by then and felt some little frog kicks in my stomach at the sound of it.

"Armando, I wasn't kidding in there about you being in my skit," she said when she caught up with me, a little out of breath. "Seriously, how about it?" Alysse raised and lowered her eyebrows a couple of times, but then added more quietly, leaning in my direction, "I mean, it's not as if this is really going anywhere. I don't know what nutcase nominated me, but everybody knows it's just a big joke. Me, homecoming queen? It's kind of like writing in Will Ferrell for U.S. president. Who would vote for a goof-off, huh?" She smiled impishly, a dimple appearing that I'd never noticed before. "Should we ask Mr. Thorndike if he thinks I should be homecoming queen?"

"I think you'd make a really good homecoming queen," I heard myself say.

My statement seemed to catch her off guard. "Oh. Oh, well, thanks, Kendall-Wendall, that's a pretty nice thing to say." But almost immediately she reached over and started patting me on the back. "I owe ya big time fer that, cowpoke! Better yet, put yer lucre where yer yacker is and come to practice. And hey, bring any western gear you might have tonight to Molly's. We're meeting at seven-thirty. That should give you time to do some homework. Don't stress over the gear, though. Tyron-eo says he's got a bunch of stuff and so does Fallon-eo, as in John. I'm bringing a bunch as well." And she grinned again as she backed away from me in the direction she'd come from. "You!" she said, pointing at me again. "I need YOU in my skit!"

I lifted my hand to protest, but by that time she was already well down the hall. "No, seriously, I can't do that," I was saying to myself.

Chapter Nine

I still to this day don't know how Allyson got me up on that stage. Okay, I guess I do know. Hokey as it sounds, she believed in me. Alysse honestly thought I was hilarious. And okay, what high school kid doesn't dream of that breakaway moment when he's up there getting applause or cheers or, even better, laughs. Alysse's comment that she wasn't homecoming queen material may also have sparked something in me.

But now, as I moved with the rest of the cowpokes across the wooden floorboards, I was seriously questioning my judgment. Sure, I had done things in front of people before. In church, for instance, I said the prayer on the sacrament almost every other week, thanks to the short supply of priests, and I have to say I felt loved even when I flubbed up and had to repeat a prayer. I'd also given a fairly decent talk from the pulpit only a few weeks before, and even though I had been scared to the core, everybody had made a big deal about it, which was why I had agreed once again to play the trombone at the next ward activity. But that was *church*, where people were required to love you. This was high school, and I did my best to avoid looking at what appeared to be thousands of faces in the auditorium below us. Luckily, there were quite a few others up there on the stage with me in similar getups: hats, vests, bandannas, and so forth. If it hadn't been for the fact that we were also riding stick horses, we might have looked impressive.

We deposited our "horses" at the fake fence near the rear of the stage, then headed to our positions, looking as cowboylike as possible. Tyrone, who was sporting some crazy red boots and an old felt hat, was shoplifting the show with his extremely exaggerated bowlegged walk. If it hadn't been for Alysse, Tyrone probably would have filled the top slot as Hollenda's star jester. The guy had worn his own share of costumes and had made a great mayor in *The Music Man*. Even though he was really hamming things up now, I couldn't cough up even a gurgle of a chuckle at his antics. I was too busy trying not to bump into anyone as I moved to my spot. It didn't help much at all that I'd almost immediately spotted Ren Jensen and his chronies, including Bret Nuswander and Nate Manicox, on the front row leaning back in their seats as if daring me to make a fool of myself.

After I got situated between Tallulah and John Fallon, who was one of the school's yell leaders, I frantically reviewed the words to my small part. It was only a line or two, but I wondered why in the world I'd said I would do a speaking part.

My palms sweaty, my mouth dry, I moved along with the rest, doing my best to stay screened from the audience, especially the front row. When one of the other cowpokes moved forward or backward slightly, I would catch a glimpse of faces, and a wave of queasiness would follow.

But when Alysse lunged onto the stage in a hat that had to be as wide as she was tall, looking like she'd just stepped out of a Looney Tune cartoon, my upper torso jerked with surprise and then began to vibrate like a Jacuzzi. Those around me on the stage had similar reactions, snorting and coughing, and audience members erupted as well. Alysse lifted her hand, palm up, in mock innocence with a "What's-wrong-I-dress-like-this-every-day" expression.

When she shouted "Howdeee!" in a high nasal tone, the air I'd managed so far to hold in exploded from my nose and mouth. By the time Alysse galloped toward us on her broom-handle steed, I was laughing outright, and with each lunge of my chest, my fear fell from me like gobs of dried mud. Laughter, I discovered that day, is one great fear-buster.

But laughter can also make it very hard to get out your lines. Parker Teal was up first. Alysse did a huge, oversized twist and pointed to him to indicate that it was his turn. Poor Parker sputtered like a plugged faucet. She did another twist, this time pointing at Parker sideways with both index fingers as she looked forward, which made him snort even more. Alysse tapped her foot with exaggeration, her eyes raised. Then she lay down on her side and pointed to Parker with a foot. When Parker still couldn't get it out, Alysse said his lines for him, moving his hands as if he were a puppet. The students really liked that.

John Fallon, who could normally blast it out, had just as hard a time coughing up his lines and went completely limp when

Alysse pretended *he* was a puppet—to the point that he fell over and lay on his back, his chest heaving. Even Tyrone, who'd had lots of practice containing himself on the stage, couldn't seem to keep it together, and Alysse had to cover for him as well.

Now it was my turn, and I gasped for breath and wiped my eyes, fully expecting Alysse to bail me out too. But when Alysse pulled me forward and said, "Come on, Deputy Chuckles, give us your reason for voting for Allyson Pringle!" I caught something: a subtle but pleading look on her face. Although she was putting on a good show, Alysse, I could tell, wasn't all that excited at the prospect of performing the entire skit by herself. I swallowed in an effort to get control, managed to pull in a breath, and then willed myself to get out the words: " . . . voting fer Allyson Pringle cuz she's . . ." That was as far as I got. I paused, lowered my head, snorted again, took another breath, lifted my head, and tried once more: "Cuz she's . . ."

"Yer makin' me nervous now, pardner," Alysse blared out. "Cuz she's what?"

I took another gasp and finally pushed it through: "Cuz she's the best durn cowgal in these-here parts."

"Wahoo!" shouted Alysse. Then, possibly out of relief that somebody had finally gotten out some lines, she jumped into the air, her feet turned up. The second she landed, she pointed at me, indicating I was to follow.

Caught up in the moment, the laughter of the audience, the craziness, I, Kendall Archer, did just that. But we hadn't rehearsed anything like it, and, fearful that I would land on my right leg, which sometimes gave me a little trouble even back then, I stumbled, but only a little. I did lose my hat, though, and after picking it up, I lifted my hand. "Lemme try that again," I said with a nasal tone and what I hoped resembled a western drawl. Had I really just said that?

"He sez he's takin' another shot at it," Allyson let the audience know.

As the students quieted down, I took a step or two to gain momentum and then jumped into the air once again, this time with both feet out and up. I'd had many a slam-dunk contest with my brother, and I have to say I got up there pretty high. The instant I landed (making sure most of the weight was on my better leg) I lifted both hands in victory. The students went crazy. "Wahoo!" several shouted.

Looking amazed and amused, Alysse pointed at me, grinning and nodding. "Musta got you mixed up. You must be Deputy Chuckles' twin brother, Jumpin' Jack Jehosafats! We'll call you *JJ and J.*"

I snorted along with the others at this nickname as Alysse moved toward Tallulah. I suspected that my making it through *my* part helped her spit out hers as well. And then the others who still had lines found the control to get their parts out.

Next, Alysse announced that we would all be doing a "clip clop" dance. You need to know your limitations, and I was happy to move to my position on the back row, where I mostly just bobbed my head in rhythm. We'd only practiced as a group once, but I got the impression, by the students' reaction, that we were looking pretty good or at least that it didn't really matter if we didn't.

Tyrone got big cheers during a little solo stick-riding, which consisted of his jumping over his stick horse handle several times. The guy was agile. "Old Ty is horsin' around again," Alysse said. She turned toward the rest of us then and said, "Next?" Since I had already participated, I felt no concern as Alysse surveyed the group. But suddenly she headed in my direction. What was she doing? The next thing I knew, she was pulling me out from behind John Fallon. "Come on, Jumpin' Jack, yer turn agin."

I'd *had* my turn! But Alysse was insistent, and soon there I was front and center. Since I wasn't into stick riding, and since it appeared she wasn't going to let this go, I did all I could think of to do. I jumped again. Holding my "horse" in a vertical position alongside me, we rose into the air. After we landed—my knee luckily cooperating again—I had both of us bow (me and the "horse," that is).

"Wahoo!" several more shouted, as classmates really clapped and laughed this time, a few even standing to get a better view.

"And it's JJ and J," said Alysse, "at it again!" There was a delayed reaction to the initials. With one last "yee-haw," Alysse galloped off the stage. The rest of us quickly followed, Tyrone lifting his hat. "Yee-haw! Vote for Alysse!"

"Yee-haw!" I heard myself repeat.

Ours was the last skit, and as we met offstage, laughing and giving each other high fives, I immediately looked for Allyson, hungry to get that pat on the back I deserved. But as the others congratulated themselves, I noticed that Alysse was standing alone near the curtain, a strange, almost terrified look on her face. And then Alysse turned toward us and said something that would have knocked us right off our stick horses had we still been riding them. "Thanks for your help and support, guys. That was terrific. Too terrific. I gotta go back out there and tell them not to vote for me."

"What? What did she say?" Tyrone stared at her in confusion as the others turned toward her almost in unison. "What'd you say?" She had all their attention now.

"Look, you did so well that now I'm afraid I might win, and the truth is, I just realized I really can't be homecoming queen. That wouldn't work."

"What do you *mean*, you can't be homecoming queen?" said John. "We just busted our butts so you could be homecoming queen!" In reality John had been lying on the stage floor laughing for most of the skit.

"No, Alysse, come on, noooo," Tallulah pleaded, reaching for her arm.

"Sorry," Alysse said, pulling away and edging toward the stage. "I've just decided. I'm going to ask everybody to vote for Charlotte Climpton instead of me." And with that she pushed open the curtain and shouted, " 'Scuse me! Hold it, folks! Hold yer horses!"

"Charlotte?" John's mouth remained open as we heard Alysse saying, "Yesiree, if you had any inklin' to be votin' fer me, I ask you to vote for Charlotte Climpton, who deserves being queen a big heap more'n I do after the year she's had!" Adding a *yee-haw*, she exited the stage on the side opposite us, yelling, "Wahoo, Charlotte!"

Other than the echo of the microphone, the auditorium was silent. Everyone, it appeared, was as surprised as we were. On the other hand, we were also all well aware of Charlotte Climpton's challenges because the school had raised money the Christmas before to help pay for her surgeries. I didn't begrudge Charlotte anything, and I don't think anyone else did either. It was just that this was unexpected. As members of the audience seemed to be digesting what had just happened, I didn't so much as blink. Finally we heard a heavy buzz and then, at last, some applause.

"What'd she do that for?" Tyrone snarled.

On the first row I saw Ren Jensen jerk his head toward Nate Manicox with what looked like a similar reaction. Not me. I pulled off my too-small cowboy hat and smiled in awe through the curtain. "She only takes the character roles," I explained to Tallulah, who was peeking through the curtain with me. "She never goes for the leading lady parts."

Chapter Ten

It's amazing how much attention a couple of leaps in a skit will get a guy. The rest of that day, people I hardly knew were greeting me in the halls with, "Hey, Jumpin' Jack," or "Howdy, JJ and J!" After school Artie Cananbella, a part-time rapper I tutored whenever he felt like showing up, wanted to hear all about the skit before we dug into business math. "You really think The Pringle was serious about us not voting for her? Because I wouldn't mind seeing old Alysse win the homecoming thing," said the guy everybody called "Tough Artie." Apparently even he was starstruck.

A few hours later, at the joint Young Men and Young Women service activity in the ward, Arnold's sisters Ella and Bella rushed me like I was a rock star. "You were soooooo funny in Allyson Pringle's skit!" chirped close-to-six-foot Ella, who had the same featherweight hair as her brother.

"Totally funny!" agreed Bella, whose booming voice never

seemed to match her five-foot frame. "But when Alysse came out and said that she wanted everybody to vote for Charlotte, I was like . . ." Bella dropped open her jaw.

"Me too," said Ella, patting down her bangs, then pulling out the little spray bottle she always carried to give them a few quick squirts.

"I think it surprised a lot of people," I said.

"I can't wait to find out what happens," said Bella.

Ella added such an energetic "me too" that I jerked back in mock surprise, even though I was feeling the same way. It was why I'd been looking around anxiously for Arnold. I happened to know, since he'd talked about little else, that he would be at the homecoming dance with Dora Eccles, a tall, skinny girl from his study class.

"So where's your bro?" I asked the twins, trying not to sound too anxious.

"He went thataway," said Bella in a not-that-lame attempt to mimic my western drawl in the skit.

"Okay," I said more eagerly than I'd planned. "Thanks, umm, pardner." Ella, who amused easily, giggled happily as Bella added her foghorn laugh that echoed through the scout room like a bass drum.

◎

"Hey, listen, you gotta do me a favor," I told my friend as soon as I found him hauling some of the bags of donations down the hall.

Arnold acknowledged me with a lift of his head and I grabbed the bag he was dragging behind him. "Sure. What do you need?"

"You gotta call me tomorrow night after the dance and tell me everything that happens, okay?" I said quietly but intensely.

Readjusting a box he was balancing on his hip, Arnold smiled a little too smugly. "You mean let you know whether Allyson wins homecoming queen?"

"Yeah, that and the rest of it." I recognized the irony myself. This time I was asking *him* for a play-by-play. *None of this "you had to be there" stuff,* I even felt like saying. Now one of those little hidden cameras or recorders didn't seem like such a bad idea.

"Hey, you coulda been there in person, you know," Arnold reminded me. "You coulda gone with The Pringle herself. You coulda gone with the queen! Well, I mean, unless she has her way and Charlotte wins queen."

"Don't start that stuff again," I moaned. Arnold had insinuated before that Alysse liked me as more than just a friend. "Join the real world, okay?" Even if I'd been in the market for a girlfriend, which I wasn't, Alysse had her pick of the Hollenda central stairs kind of guys.

I think Arnold had more to say, possibly something about how I always underestimated myself, but as we came to the door of the multipurpose room, Brother Wanslot was describing conditions in the *real* real world—the lack of adequate supplies, even safe drinking water. Shame filled me as he described the conditions of the orphans in Somalia who didn't even have the most basic essentials. Here the biggest concern of my life seemed to be what would be happening at some high school dance when there were little kids out there struggling to stay alive. How shallow was I?

Apparently pretty shallow. "So, you won't forget to contact me after the dance, right?" I reminded Arnold a little later as we deposited toothbrushes and toothpaste packets in the grooming kits we would be sending off.

"Double promise!" sniffed my friend, a term he'd used since we were eight or nine. To my relief, he skipped the part where he spat on his palms and slapped mine.

The following night Arnold was true to his double promise even without the spit to bind it. He called me on my cell, which I had put on vibrate and stuck in my armpit when I went to bed so it would wake me up no matter what time he called. But what he told me left me speechless. It was neither Alysse nor Charlotte but Bluebell Wilcox who'd been voted queen.

"Yeah, everybody was pretty surprised," said Arnold. He speculated then that neither Allyson nor Charlotte had taken the top spot because the votes were split between them. His date, Dora, he went on, didn't think Bluebell would have had a chance if she hadn't changed her name, taken up the electric guitar, and painted blue stripes in her hair the previous summer. "But you had to be happy for Bluebell," said Arnold, as ever the peace-on-earth-goodwill-to-men kind of guy. "You could tell she totally didn't expect to win. Luckily, she got a good reaction and some decent applause. But, mate, you shoulda heard them when Alysse was announced first runner-up."

"So Alysse got first attendant?" I pulled myself up a little. This was more like it.

"Yeah, and the place went crazy. She was about the only one there who didn't act excited when her name was called. But she was sure happy a few seconds later when they announced Charlotte as second attendant. She went into another cheerleader routine and jumped on a chair and got everybody chanting *Charlotte! Charlotte!*"

"So Charlotte got second attendant." I was still smiling widely.

"That's right," Arnold confirmed. "And if you thought Bluebell was excited, you shoulda seen Charlotte. She was beyond excited. The girl was beaming to the ceiling. She looked nice, too. Somebody'd done up her hair, and she had on a good dress."

Picturing Charlotte all fixed up nicely choked me up a little, but by the time Arnold told me that Alysse had once again come in costume, this time as "Alice in Wonderland" complete with the bow, I was giggling like a stage mother.

"So it sounds like it turned out to be an all-around good dance," I said happily. "Maybe you're right. Maybe I should have gone just to be there. I'm not necessarily talking about with Alysse," I added quickly. "But I probably could have found some-one to go with." I think maybe at that moment I *was* secretly hop-ing Arnold would say something again about how Alysse would have gone with me if I'd asked her, but instead there was a long pause. "Arnold?"

"There's probably one more thing I should tell you," he said far too quietly.

"Okay, what's that?"

"It was hard to tell for sure, but I think she might have come with our old friend Ren Jensen."

"Ren Jensen?" My stomach did a rollover.

"Yup. Either that or they hooked up when they got there. And even if they're not an item now, they soon may be, considering the way he was nuzzling her neck during the last dance. Sorry, mate."

"Why should I care?" I reacted. "I told you, Alysse and I are just friends, remember? I've always told you that."

"Well, you know . . ."

"Yeah, yeah." I sighed. There was no point trying to fool my friend. I wasn't even doing a good job fooling myself. "Okay, you're right. Ren Jensen isn't somebody I'd have picked for her." I rose up at this point in order to catch some air. I could still feel that extra twist Ren had given my arm the last time he'd talked his friends into trying to deposit me in the nearest trash can. It's hard to warm up to people who think you belong in the trash. But even worse—afterward, when we were all hauled into the office because some courageous hall monitor turned us in, Ren had looked straight into the eyes of Mr. Julliard, the vice principal, and sworn I had started the whole thing. He even came up with some ugly racial slurs I'd supposedly said to Nate Manicox, who's maybe a fourth of a percent African American. The guy just stood there and lied through his perfect teeth. His friends, even Nate, backed him up. Being lied about had hurt worse than the physical part of it.

After Arnold and I disconnected, I couldn't get to sleep. Ren Jensen! *Man*, living the gospel could be challenging. I had worked a long time at trying to soften my attitude toward Ren. Finally, toward the end of the previous year, I'd gotten to the point where

I didn't feel like I wanted to flatten him every time I saw him. Now, just like that, I was feeling like I might need to start all over in these efforts. Okay, I'd seen Ren and some of his friends hanging around with Alysse once or twice, but so many people hung around her that it hadn't really made an impression. But now . . .

Did Alysse know what this guy was like? I chuckled bitterly. Hey, what did I expect? Ren was captain of the varsity football team and had been voted "hottest guy" the year before by the Hollenda High Girls Association. Maybe Alysse wasn't so different from the mindless girls in our school who seemed to go for the nasty-tempered, bad-guy type. I huffed out another bitter laugh. I was glad, really glad I'd decided not to have a girlfriend until after my mission! They were all alike.

But then something smacked me across the brain with a two-by-four. It was none of my business who Alysse chose to go to a dance with or run around with! She and I had fun kidding around together and she was nice to me—but she was nice to a lot of people, including some of the underdogs of the school. What made me think I was special? At that point a big "I" for *Insecure* might as well have reemerged on my chest (never having completely disappeared) as I even wondered if she considered me one of those underdogs. She'd made it clear that she thought I was "different," hadn't she?

I sniffed with self-disgust. I'd been making this big thing out of Alysse's paying attention to me and joking around with me when that was what she did for a living. I was a pitiful idiot, worse even than Arnold, to be this starstruck about a girl who just happened to be funny and nice and, okay, really cute. Maaaaaan, I'd even had Arnold call me in the middle of the night about her! What a loser I was! Didn't I have enough to think about and do? I was behind in my homework because of all this homecoming stuff, and there was the wedding coming up. And hadn't I vowed I would study the lessons in *Preach My Gospel* and memorize the recommended scriptures before I got my call? Yup, I definitely had better things to think about and do. It was time to get my priorities straight.

"Hey, Duck, old boy, I think I just got a reality check," I told my dog, who was sitting by my feet, his brown eyes alert. Lucky Duck, who was pretty sensitive to my moods, let out a little *woof* of empathy and beat his tail just once against the wood floor.

Chapter Eleven

In third period on Monday, I tried my best to act normal and even congratulated Alysse in Spanish again, this time on being chosen homecoming first attendant. But it didn't take her long to pick up on the fact that I wasn't the same upbeat Kendall-Armando she'd been joking around with just a few days before. I tend to be pretty transparent, and what I was really feeling was apparently oozing through my skin. "¿Qué pasa?" she asked during conversation time, adopting her chipmunk-Elmo voice. "Is Kenny-Wenny in a funky-wunky?"

"Why do you ask that?"

"Cuz Kenny act sad." Allyson lifted her index finger and widened her eyes. "Alysse help Kenny feel better!" With this, she began plowing through her Minnie Mouse bag until she found a giant plaid hanky.

"Uhhhh, no, thanks," I said, pulling back.

"For Kenny-Wenny," she insisted, lifting the hanky toward my nose.

"Sorry, I'm not blowing my nose into your hanky. Or is it a small tablecloth?" I was trying to sound disgusted, so it bothered me that I was on the verge of laughing again.

"Kenny-Wenny—oops, I mean Armando-Warando—blow nose in hanky," she insisted, moving the cloth closer.

"Go away!" I said, pulling back. Alysse continued trying to catch my nose. "Seriously," I said, still trying not to laugh. Alysse could even make a person enjoy being annoyed.

Finally, I gave up and grabbed the hanky. "Fine, I'll blow my nose in that whatever it is, but only if you promise to quit calling me Kenny-Wenny."

"Oh, so sorry, big Kendall," she responded, her voice lower.

I sighed, lifted my eyes, and held the hanky to my nose, pretending to honk.

"Aw, come on, big guy, you can do better than that!" she said, sounding more like a storm trooper now.

"HONK!" I bulged out my eyes for comic effect. Those around us were involved and laughing as well by this time. Carlin turned with a half grin and Daphne giggled from a couple of seats away. Rhonda looked over, shaking her head in amusement.

"Oh my goodness," Alysse cried, pulling back, "hold the levees! It's a tidal wave!"

Alvarez came into the room right then, and I was half afraid Alysse would ask our teacher how to say *honk* in Spanish. I shook my head but chuckled as I rolled my eyes. How can you stay in a "funky-wunky" when somebody has you honk into a huge plaid hanky?

For the rest of the week, Alysse paid even more attention to me than she had before homecoming. I tried really hard not to let it affect me when, after she saw me in the hall on Wednesday, she pulled away from the Beal twins and Lindsey Bell and John Fallon and walked a ways down the AB hall with me. Again she had me laughing. That next week and the week after I continued to get special treatment, and the following Friday, when I decided to show up for a few minutes at Hollenda's annual Halloween Bash, I was flattered to the bone marrow when Alysse, who was decked out as a humongous potted plant, left the group she was with and waddled over to compliment me (sarcastically) on the aluminum foil star I'd made to go with the same old cowboy outfit I'd worn in the skit. "Big effort," she joked.

Then, even though I ended up with one group and she with another, which included a vampire I guessed was none other than my old friend Ren, she made it a point to waddle back over when she saw me leaving—no small chore in her hula hoop flowerpot. "Let me guess: homework!"

"You got it."

"Well, then, here's one for the road, Sheriff Party Poopster," she said, and, with Ren looking on, she handed me a purple petal from her wrist.

It's funny how little things can mean a lot. I kept that petal on the bulletin board in my room until I left on my mission.

The following Monday as well, Alysse paid special attention to me. "If you'd told me you were coming as a sheriff to the Halloween Bash, I would have loaned you the nice big hat I wore in the homecoming skit," she said.

"I thought you gave that back to Yosemite Sam," I shot back happily.

"Oh wait, you're right," she joked. "I did, didn't I?"

I was doing better now. I'd decided not to worry about things I had no control over. There wasn't much I could do about the fact that Arnold had turned out to be right and that it looked like Alysse was hanging with Ren pretty much regularly now. But as far as she and I were concerned, whatever was going on with Ren didn't seem to be making a difference in her attitude and friendship toward me. We still clicked like a good lock when it came to humor. Even better, every once in a while Alysse let her mask slip a little as we talked about assignments or things going on in the state or the world. She even confided in me now and then— nothing major, just challenges in her school office, for instance, an assignment I could tell she seemed to really relish, but which she took far more seriously than anyone would have guessed.

As for Ren, I tried to convince myself that people really do change and that maybe he was an okay guy now and that it wasn't up to me to judge him any more than I judged those who chose to go the tattoo route. People grow up, I decided. I even told myself that it was good that Allyson had a boyfriend, regardless of who it was, so that I wouldn't let my imagination carry me to some never-never land where I couldn't and shouldn't go anyway.

Chapter Twelve

I don't know how Allyson found out that my birthday was on November 20th, but a few minutes into Spanish that day, she shocked the socks off me by calling right out, "Señor Alvarez, we need to wish Armando here *Feliz Cumpleaños!* How do you sing the birthday song in Spanish?"

I lifted my head, my lips rounding, then glanced at our teacher for his reaction as several class members clapped and laughed.

Even though Alysse was pushing the envelope again, good old Alvarez smiled and agreed to sing an Americanized version. "*Cumpleaños, Feliz, Cumpleaños, Feliz, Cumpleaños, Cumpleaños, Cumpleaños Feliz!*" What can I say? The guy was cool.

"Piece of cake," said Alysse.

"Cake? No . . . *pastel* or *torta*," said Alvarez. "*Sí, es fácil.*" Then I assumed he was telling her to do the honors, because Alysse happily jumped out of her seat, rose to her toes, and led the class in the birthday song with great enthusiasm.

We were at least twenty minutes into the class period by the time we got to our regular curriculum, and I've wondered since how Alvarez filled up the time in his other classes that didn't have Alysse in them.

"So how old did you turn today?" Alysse asked after class. She was looking at me kind of sideways, "Umm, *cuantos . . . años . . . tienes?*"

"*Dieciocho,*" I answered, still reeling from all the unexpected attention I'd just received. I'd never in my life had that many people sing "Happy Birthday" to me.

"So you're eighteen, huh? Legal age. That's what I thought, but you never know. For all I know you could have skipped a grade. That wouldn't surprise me."

I felt an urge to argue that point because people have always considered me smarter than I really am, but decided against it.

Alysse looked around, her voice quieter. "So, does that mean you're old enough to go to a dance? I heard Mormons can't go to dances until they reach a certain age." Without taking her eyes from me, Alysse folded her vocabulary sheet into her Spanish book, which she carefully slid into her Minnie Mouse bag. "What's the magic coming-out age?"

"That'd be sixteen," I said to the notebook I was pushing into my backpack. Where, I wondered, was she heading with this?

"So how many dances have *you* been to?"

Now she was stepping into some sensitive territory. Kip especially gave me a bad time about my lack of social experience. That wasn't to say I hadn't been *invited* to a few dances. I'd *almost* gone to the girl's preference dance the year before with Marin Kilpack,

Abe Stanley's cousin, but she'd come down with mono just a few days before. "Hey, you just saw me at the Halloween Bash, didn't you?"

Alysse cleared her throat with exaggeration. "The Halloween Bash? Sorry, Kendall-Armando, but even if you'd stayed more than four and a half minutes, the Halloween Bash wouldn't count. I'm talking about real, official dances."

"Well, in that case . . . umm, let me think." I began to count on my fingers in mock concentration, but then curved my index finger and thumb into a zero and lifted it.

"Exactly what I was afraid of." Alysse scrunched her mouth to one side and nodded. "Well, you know what? If you haven't been to an official dance, I'm going to see to it personally that you go to the Winter Formal!"

"I'm really not that into dancing," I objected quickly and with concern. "You might have noticed that when we put on the skit. And what about . . . I mean, wouldn't I need to be somebody's . . ."

"Date? Yes, of course. You'd be going with *me*, silly. You'd be my date."

She laughed merrily when I sucked in my breath with surprise. For the first time since we'd become friends, I didn't have a comeback of any kind. Why was she doing this? "You betcha, it'll be you and me," she continued. But then she hesitated ever so slightly. "So, how about it?"

"You're just giving me a bad time now," I said, looking around. "Is this a setup or something?" I meant what I was saying. I figured it had to be one of her practical jokes. But only Dennis Craig was still in his seat, and he wasn't laughing. Neither was anyone else.

Lakeesha was talking to James Domrose on the other side of the room, and only a few others were still in the classroom. The rest had headed out.

"No, I'm serious," said Alysse, and I could tell by her voice and a couple of extra blinks that she was.

I pulled my backpack up to my shoulder, feeling all the symptoms of a good old-fashioned panic attack. I was twelve or thirteen again, stuttering and sputtering. "So, will there be others? Will there be a group?"

Alysse chuckled. "Aw, yer skeered you might be alone with little Alysse, ain't ya?" she said, slipping again into her western drawl—or was it her hillbilly accent? "Well, you can rest yer little mind. There's a big whoppin' group of us goin'. You know Dee Dee and Caleb Sweeney, and our old buddy Rhonda and Jake over there." She looked toward the door where the happy couple were laughing. "And Dansco and Tallulah, and, let's see, Rich and one of the Beal twins. He can't decide which one. And Lindsey's going with Carlin. You know Carlin." Of course I did. Even if he hadn't been in Spanish with us, I would have known who he was. In fact, Alysse had just named the people in the school everybody knew— class officers, athletes, the stars who hung out on the central stairs. "Dansco" was her nickname for Dan Scoville, the senior class president, and she brought him up again. "Dansco knows somebody, and he thinks he can get us a limo," she said. "We'll be cruisin' in style and you won't even need to pick me up. You're on the way, so we can just swing by."

I lifted my head at this information. "I wouldn't need to

drive?" Since I really didn't have a car I would want anybody to actually get into, this information seemed significant.

"And wait'll you hear this!" said Alysse as she glanced toward the rear door at Rhonda, who'd switched to John Fallon and was flashing her ultra-whitened teeth at him. "Since this would be your first dance and since I'm guessing you traumatize easily, I'm actually planning to come in a regular formal dress." She pulled back and nodded. "How do you like that, huh? Jingle Pringle in a normal formal."

"And not a costume?" I recognized this as big. "Isn't that a first?"

"It is."

"And you'd do this just because I'm so conservative?"

"You guessed it. So how about it?" Alysse paused then and waited, trying not to look concerned about how I planned to answer. But the slight flicker that I'd learned to recognize indicated otherwise.

"I can't believe you haven't already been asked by somebody else," I said, stalling. What I was really wondering was why she wasn't going with Ren Jensen and what was going on there. In the latest "Who's Who" column of *The Dutchman's Herald*, our school paper, Alysse and Ren had been listed as *the* couple to watch.

Alysse seemed to know what I was thinking and she suddenly turned serious. "You'd actually be helping me out." There was another flicker of something I couldn't distinguish, but soon she grinned and went into another routine. "And hey, y'all Mormons are 's'pose' to help people out, ain't ya?"

I lifted my chin. "So how would I be helping you out?"

She glanced toward the back door where Tallulah had joined Jake, John, and Rhonda. Rhonda made a comment to the group and glanced in impatiently. Alysse raised and lowered her eyebrows a few times at them, then turned back to me, her grin wavering slightly. "You just would."

I glanced toward the back door myself, hesitated, but then took a deep breath. "Okay, well . . ."

"Well . . . ?" She flashed her amazingly turquoise eyes at me.

"Since you say Mormons are 's'pose' to help people out, I don't have much of a choice, do I?"

"Not what I'd call the most highly flattering answer, but seriously, you'll really go, then?"

"*Sí, Señorita*, I'd be, ummm, *emocionado* to go to the dance with you." It was one of our vocabulary words.

"*Gracias, Señor.*" She bowed and smiled widely. I wondered at this point just how badly I was blushing. But then I noticed that Alysse's neck was flushed and her cheeks were rosier than usual.

I have to admit that the rest of the day was a blur. I had so little to say at lunch that Parry asked me if I was okay.

"Yeah, yeah, I'm fine," I muttered evasively. Parry was a nice enough dude, but he talked a little too much and I wasn't sure I was ready to unplug what had just happened quite yet. In fact, I was kind of glad for once that Arnold had second lunch instead of first because he always seemed to be able to read my face even when something not all that big was up. And this was big. Oh, yeah. So big I was having a really hard time believing that what had just happened really had, and I ate my peanut-butter sandwich as I looked around the cafeteria with a robot-like stare.

I don't think it hit me full force until orchestra that I, Kendall-Wendall, alias Jumpin' Jack, Armando, Archer, Kenny, and whatever, was really going to a dance, my first ever, with Allyson Delilah Eleanor Penelope Pringle (at least she claimed those were all her names), the funnest and funniest girl in the school. In other words, this was serious! I considered it a lucky thing that the Thanksgiving break was coming up. I had the feeling that I might once again be putting off the science project I'd planned to start on that weekend. I wondered if I could maybe Google a complete list of things a guy needs to do to get ready for a dance. I winced and blew out air as I realized I might finally be calling my Aunt Betty about dance lessons, something I had managed to avoid thus far in my life. She and my mother would be ecstatic. I smiled as I pictured how my old buddy Arnold would react to my news. Arnold would freak!

But then Ren and some of his friends strutted by the orchestra room door heading for who knew where, and I froze. Within seconds the excitement was seeping back in, however, this time swelling over, and I lifted my trombone and blasted happily into it.

Chapter Thirteen

Other than the fact that the lessons with Aunt Betty hadn't gone so well, by the night of the dance I considered myself fairly well prepared. I'd assumed that because of the wedding I wouldn't be able to count on my family members for much, but when I finally got around to telling them about the dance, they came through for me big time. Mom, after I practically had to get her a paper bag to stop her hyperventilating at the news, immediately raced to the hall closet and pulled out Kip's old tux, which she'd been planning to shorten for me to wear at my sister's reception anyway, and almost ran it to the sewing room.

Lynette brought over one of Josh's formal shirts and his black bow tie and reminded me not to fidget. Dad helped me find some cuff links and let me know the same rules applied to me as had applied to my siblings. Since it was his belief that the Spirit was harder to tune into after midnight, I was to be back within seconds—okay, minutes—after the clock struck twelve. Twelve-fifteen at the latest. Kip advised me to loosen up and have a good time but to watch the hormones, and he recommended a good antiperspirant. Even Monica called from Utah to tell me to make sure there was nothing in my teeth, not to overdo the aftershave, and to stand up straight. "Just because you're getting married doesn't mean you need to start sounding like Mom," I said.

After he calmed down, Arnold, who might as well have been family, even offered some advice. "Don't pick the corsage up too early," he suggested. "Five days before is too early. The petals fall off." I had the feeling he was speaking from experience.

Along with dance steps I practiced each night in front of the old, broken, full-length mirror I'd pulled in from the storage room, I rehearsed possible things I could say and how I could say them. So yeah, I *thought* I was prepared.

But when Allyson rustled into our entryway all shiny and shimmery, her hair pulled up in a fancy new style, looking—I'll say it—*beautiful*, I totally lost my emotional footing and started rolling downhill fast. "Om, this is Malice," I heard myself say. Mortified, I squeezed my eyes shut. "Sorry, I mean Mallyson." I stopped and took a breath. "I mean Allyson." I moaned, then shook my head with self-disgust. "And Alysse, this is my mom and not my *om*."

As Alysse chuckled, my mother let out a small puff of relief. "Gosh, I thought *Malice* was an awfully unusual name. Even *Mallyson* is different. But now that he reminds me, of course I knew your name was Allyson or Alysse because Kendall has said your name many, many times this past week or two."

One *many* would have been plenty.

"And that looks like a beautiful dress," my mother continued, too eagerly. "Is the top the same red plaid taffeta as the skirt?" Thanks to the wedding, Mom was really into dresses lately. I hoped she wouldn't try to feel the fabric.

"No, the top's red velvet," Alysse said, lifting a soft, shawl-type covering.

I closed my eyes just in case there might be skin. I'd seen some of the formal dresses on those TV pageants and awards shows, and it wasn't uncommon for them to have large sections missing. In fact, it was one of the things I'd worried about. Alysse wasn't LDS, after all, and I had wondered what she would consider a "normal formal." I opened my eyes just in time to catch a glimpse of Allyson's nicely narrow and completely covered waist.

"It looks like a lovely dress for a lovely girl. A *very* lovely girl." Mom looked at me accusingly. "Kendall didn't tell us how darling you are."

"I don't know about that, but your Christmas decorations are sure beautiful, Mrs. Archer," Alysse said then, quickly and skillfully shifting the attention away from herself.

It was the perfect thing to say to my mother, who had hurriedly gotten out the Christmas boxes just that morning.

Fortunately, before my mother could go into too much detail concerning the decorations, and even before she started in on the wedding (her favorite topic lately), my father made his appearance. *Un*fortunately, he was wearing the falling-apart work pants my mother had asked him not to wear again until she repaired the zipper. I nailed the introduction this time, though, and Dad seemed impressed with Alysse, especially when she brought up the previous evening's Pistons game. She even got the old man chuckling a little. Unlike her date, Alysse was doing and saying all the right things.

Since they had been raised in the pre-feminist era, I had already explained to my parents about the limo and why Alysse was picking me up instead of vice versa. When Alysse pulled out a boutonnière for me, I quickly grabbed her corsage from the hall table. She politely made a fuss over it and, a short while later, after Mom located the camera, we found ourselves out on the fairly good-sized front porch. It wasn't as cold as it had been, which was good, because the limo that Dansco had promised to rent, and that I'd pulled a good chunk of change from my emergency fund to help pay for, was nowhere in sight. "Either they're playing a trick on us, or they've gone to pick up Lindsey," Alysse speculated. "She lives just a couple of miles from here."

"Okay." I pulled nervously on my bow tie until I remembered my sister's suggestion that I not fidget. Jerking my hand from my tie, I let it drop to my side like a dead weight. Now, I realized, would be a good time to say one of the things I had practiced in the mirror. I frantically tried to recall some of the witticisms, but the mind is a funny thing. I couldn't remember one phrase, not a single word. Nothing. It was just as well, since I doubt I would have gotten the words out anyway with my teeth going at it like castanets. Why, I wondered, was I reacting this way? Why was I so intent on proving I was a complete dork? Hey, I was a senior! I was eighteen! Wasn't I finally beyond that? And, more important, wasn't this *Alysse*? I needed to remember that this was Alysse, the good friend I talked to and joked with every day in school. It was just that Alysse was looking and acting so *un*Alysse-like.

Alysse apparently felt the need to say something as well. "So, um . . ." we spat out simultaneously.

"You first," I insisted quickly, mainly because I had already forgotten what I'd planned to say.

"I was just going to say that I hope you didn't tell your parents that I went to homecoming as a Viking last year."

"I don't think I mentioned that," I assured her, a corner of my mouth lifting ever so slightly.

"Good, because your mother already thinks I'm plenty interesting."

"Why do you say that?" I was under the impression that Alysse had been proper beyond belief.

"Well, hopefully she's clear now that my name isn't *Malice*, but I noticed her staring at my feet while your dad went to change into better pants. Maybe because I'm wearing these." Alysse lifted the hem of her shiny skirt to reveal thigh-high rubber boots.

"Are we going fishing?"

She giggled at that. "No, we're not going fishing. Yesterday afternoon I broke five toes, two on my left foot and three on my right. These boots were the only things I could get over my swollen feet."

"How on earth did you break your toes?"

"Tiny snow monsters," she said without flinching. "Thousands of little snow men and women and their even tinier children. I guess they thought my toes were alien pygmies."

The other corner of my mouth joined its partner.

"Mini snow monsters, huh? Gosh, that must have been traumatic."

"Okay, okay, maybe it wasn't quite like that."

"I kinda wondered," I joked. "So what really happened?"

"It was pretty boring, actually. This piece of scenery we were making for the holiday talent show slipped and my feet happened to be where it landed. They were so swollen this morning that I thought there for a little while I was a troll."

"Ouch," I said, feeling for her.

"There's not a whole lot you can do about broken toes," she continued. "The foot doctor gave me those big padded shoes to wear, but try wearing two of them. I was walking like this." She demonstrated.

"Kind of how you walked in the cowboy skit?" I heard myself tease.

"Pretty close," Alysse tucked in the corners of her mouth, but winced as well.

I felt guilty for making light of her injury. "So are you sure you even want to go? You could have gotten out of this, you know."

"Yeah, I know I could have gotten out of this, but maybe I didn't want to get out of it." She sidled up to me, and as she did I caught a whiff of mango with a touch of almond, a nice combination.

"Hey, it's you and me, remember?" Alysse chuckled happily again. "I'll bet you've been wanting to get out of this in the worst way. I could tell when I came to the door that you were nervous as a blue jay. But you know what? You're not getting out of this!" She grinned widely and slipped her arm through mine. "Just look at it this way: Since I have this toe problem, at least you won't need to worry about actually dancing now. That's one thing you can cross off your list."

I wondered how she knew about my list.

"I admit that might be good," I said. Then I heard myself add: "My Aunt Betty will be relieved too." Next thing I knew, I was telling Alysse about the dancing lessons. I even went into a few of the more painful details, such as the "dip" that sent Aunt Betty and me both sprawling. "Let's just say I'm pretty sure my Aunt Betty won't be recommending me to *So You Think You Can Dance.*"

Alysse thought my description of Aunt Betty and my dance lessons was so funny that she had to sniff and wipe her eyes. I was feeling a whole lot better now. My teeth had even stopped clicking. Unfortunately, my newfound confidence didn't last. Less than two minutes later, the very long and intimidating limo that I knew was filled with some of the most popular kids at the school pulled around the corner. Once again panic set in. Yeah, they seemed like nice people, but how well did I really know them? I'd heard about the stuff that could go on before and after proms. Alysse must have again read my mind, or maybe she just felt my arm stiffen. "Oh, by the way," she said, "since this is your first dance, we all decided we're going to be total Mormons tonight."

I pulled back, the smile reappearing. "And everybody's okay with that?"

"Well, Caleb wasn't so excited about it until I reminded him about your leap in my homecoming skit and that Mormons are allowed to have fun and even be funny. I even told him some of the things you've said and done in class. In fact, you really need to share what you just told me about your dance lessons. That's classic."

"Nah," I said very quickly. "You had to be there." But I was smiling along with her. I had the feeling that things might be going just fine at the Winter Wonderland dance. In fact, I had the feeling that I might even have a really good time on the first date of my life. And I did. Oh yeah, I really did.

Chapter Fourteen

As we think back on our lives, we all have those highs—experiences that stand out in our memories like lit-up farmhouses on a wide prairie. My baptism and confirmation, receiving my patriarchal blessing, being ordained to the priesthood, getting my mission call—they were some of the spiritual high points and milestones. And that's not even taking into account some of the amazing things that happened in the mission field. As far as academics, my graduation from high school was, of course, up there, and there were even a couple of academic honors. But I have to say that sitting on the sidelines at the Winter Wonderland dance with Allyson Pringle, even now, all this time later, still ranks as the social highlight of my life.

Even though Alysse and I weren't dancing and weren't even out there on the floor because of her toe problem, it felt as if we were in the center of a solar system. Classmates called and waved to us, and whole packs came over to talk and joke. For the first full hour or so, members of the group we had come with stayed to visit, taking shifts: Dansco and Tallulah, Lindsey and Carlin, Rhonda and Jake, and even Dee Dee and Caleb. As a joke, Dee Dee had rigged up a halo for Caleb and kept asking if they were acting "Mormon" enough. It turned into kind of a "Simon Says" game and an opportunity for me to share information about the Church. When Caleb, for instance, used a not-so-great word, he glanced my way quickly and said, "Oops, sorry, I'll bet that's not in your Mormon dictionary."

"I'm guessing you're right about that," I agreed, nodding slowly.

Although I sensed she was listening to everything going on, Alysse was leaning back, her legs propped up on an adjacent chair, her fishing boots well displayed. Sure enough, she got a lot of wisecracks about them. Most people, I'm sure, had no idea she'd injured herself and assumed she had just worn them for the usual reason—because she was Alysse. On the way in, she'd collected bits and pieces that had fallen from the decorations, which she stuck in her hair at odd angles like antennae. The girl just couldn't bring herself to play it straight.

"Hey, Alysse!" James Domrose shouted. Five seconds later, Bluebell Wilcox called out, "Hey, Jingle Pringle!" I was surprised when she added, "And it's JJ and J!" I was even more surprised when her date, a junior on the swimming team, added, "Hey there, Archer!"

I acknowledged them, but then let Alysse take it from there. As the evening progressed, however, I found myself coming up with one-liners myself, laughing and basking in the fun and attention right along with her. By the middle of the evening, I hardly recognized myself as the nervous kid who'd gotten his tongue twisted a few hours before.

Even Arnold and Dora stopped by to say hello a couple of times. Arnold, who'd practically done a back flip when I'd told him about my date with Alysse, was, to my relief, a little more subdued now that he was all dressed up. He would wait for Alysse to say something funny, grin at Dora, and then they'd happily take off laughing. Alysse, I couldn't help but notice, treated Arnold and Dora with the same degree of respect—or shall we say friendly lack of it—as she did Tim McKinley, our student-body president, and his date, the previous year's homecoming queen.

I didn't see Ren Jensen at the dance and wasn't exactly grieving about that. I'd done my best to avoid him the previous week or two, but Hollenda wasn't *that* big of a school, and it had been a tense period. Some of his friends were definitely there, including Bret Nuswander, who didn't look all that happy that Alysse and I were having such a good time. But everybody else seemed fine about Alysse being with somebody who not only wasn't captain of the varsity football team but wasn't even on a team of any description.

About midway into the dance, things gradually began to tone down for Allyson and me as classmates actually started dancing. We were on the opposite end of the gym from the band, and as the music slowed down, we were able to talk.

"So, have you always been self-disciplined and civilized and refined?" she asked, her smile softer than usual.

"Civilized and refined?" I was remembering the belching

contests I'd had with my brother growing up. Sure, I had definitely been called self-disciplined before, but those other two adjectives were new to me. "Is that a nice way of saying shy and quiet?"

"I wouldn't call you shy at all, especially not tonight. Okay, sometimes—and maybe compared to me."

"No, now *you* are definitely not shy."

"Oh, come on, everybody's shy sometimes." Alysse puckered her lips, lowered her head, and placed her index finger over her mouth.

I shook my head. "Sorry, I'm not buying it."

"Maybe you just don't know me that well."

I knew her better than she realized, but shy? I shook my head again. "If you're honestly shy, then you are one great actress, because you have a lot of people really fooled."

"I'm glad to hear that because that's what I want to be—an actress." She hesitated, biting her lip, then continued. "I'm not kidding. After high school I'm hoping to get into a really good drama school in New York. I have a couple in mind. Seriously, it's one of my main goals. That and Broadway."

"That doesn't surprise me."

"Really? Why?"

"Why?" Wasn't it obvious? "Umm . . . for starters, you like to wear costumes." I wasn't satisfied with my response. "And you're funny and talented. When you're up there on a stage, you own it."

She lifted her shoulders. "Wow, you really ladle it out!" But then her voice softened again. "I hope I'm somewhat talented. I mean, compared to what's in New York. I've been working at it for a long time. I've been to so many plays it'd make you dizzy, and I've memorized whole sections of scenes I wasn't even in."

"You really do love this stuff, then, huh? I mean, the character roles. So would you ever consider trying out for a lead?"

"Maybe if it were Billie Dawn in *Born Yesterday* or Princess Winnefred in *Once Upon a Mattress*."

"Because, like you say, you're shy?"

"Because I'm SHYYYYYYIE!" she belted out.

"Whoa!" I said, jerking way back.

"Go Alysse! Yes!" a couple dancing by called out. Several others turned and laughed and waved.

"Hey, Carol Burnett did it better."

"Yeah, well, I'd suggest you not try that in history."

Alysse laughed casually, even happily. "Hey, Mr. Thorndike isn't so bad. I think he and I have worked things out since that Dutch boy costume incident, don't you?"

Was she kidding? "Umm, noooo." I sincerely hoped she was joking. How could she not be aware of the way Thorndike's mouth twisted when she walked into the classroom, the way he narrowed his eyes as they followed her? I had the feeling he was just biding his time, lying in wait, so to speak, in hopes she would step over that edge she liked to walk along. I'd been meaning to have a little talk with her about the oversized earrings and headgear she'd been wearing to her classes, including history. Warn her. My eyebrows together, I opened my mouth, but Allyson was already moving on.

"So how about you?" she asked, mischievously pushing her index finger into my upper arm. "Would *you* ever try out for the lead in a play? In fact, hey!" She lifted her finger and widened her eyes. "You should try out for one of the leads in *Bye Bye Birdie.*"

Even though I wasn't planning to go anywhere near a stage again for quite a while, I'd been excited when Mr. Hammond, our orchestra teacher, had let us know that Hollenda would be presenting *Bye Bye Birdie* in the spring. Thanks to the fact that my sister Lynette had found the video at a garage sale one summer and we'd watched it possibly five hundred times, I was very familiar with the play.

"Believe me, I was doing really well just to be in your homecoming skit," I said, shaking my head like my dog after a bath. "I think that was about as much stage work as I can handle for a while. I still can't believe that was me up there. I look back and I think, *Nah, that wasn't me. That was somebody else.*"

Alysse chuckled and smiled widely, her beautiful teeth reflecting the light from the lit-up snowflakes floating near us. "Even I have to admit, those really were some amazing leaps. But hey, I figure a guy who can leap like that can probably learn to tap dance. Plus you've got that aunt thing going." She laughed again. "Aunt Betty, is it? She'd help you, right?" Alysse pursed her lips together and raised her eyebrows.

I laughed almost cheerily, but knew exactly where she was going with this and thought I'd better squelch it early. "Nuh-uh," I said. "I'm not trying out for the role of Albert Peterson." I was referring to one of the more conservative characters in *Bye Bye Birdie*, the part played by Dick Van Dyke in the movie, at least in the video version we had watched. "But I think I know who you'll be trying out for," I added quickly. "Albert's wacko mother."

Allyson's eyes turned into mini satellite dishes. "Yeah, Mama! How do you know the characters?"

I told her then about my sister's try at the Guinness record for the number of times someone watches the same video in one summer. "But don't worry, I'll be participating, just not on the stage. More like below it."

She caught on immediately. "In the orchestra? No kidding. What do you play?"

I extended my arm.

"The trombone? I love it! But hey, we could have used you in *The Music Man*."

"Seventy-six of me?"

She let out an involuntary snort. Then, smiling gently, she smoothed down her dress until the hemline slipped down over her boots, leaving only the toes showing. Looking a little vulnerable, she lifted her delicate chin in my direction. "You really do remind me of my brother, Pete. He's not like me, not the lampshade-on-the-head stuff, I mean. He has more of a dry sense of humor, like you. Oh, don't get me wrong, he can be hysterically funny, but if there's a choice, he'd rather not perform in front of too many people. Once, when I tricked him into being the MC at a function my dad was involved with, he came through big time, just like you did in my skit, and he was a hit."

I wasn't sure how flattered a guy should feel to have a girl tell him he reminded her of her brother, but I was happy she was sharing things about herself and anxious that she continue. "So, do you have other brothers and sisters, or is it just you and Pete?"

Alysse opened her mouth for a second but then shut it, as if this were a sensitive topic. She tugged at her hem, revealing green fishing boot again, but then she changed her mind and let the skirt fall back over her ankle. Lifting her chin even higher, she tilted it slightly, her smile stiffening somewhat. "I have some stepbrothers and stepsisters." Alysse ran her fingers through the loose portion of her hair in front, pulling out a piece of tinsel and staring at it as if wondering whether to continue. Finally she studied my face for a second or two. She looked around the gym, then continued. "This last time my dad got married was his sixth try, and this new wife has a couple of kids. The other stepkids along with their moms have come and gone. My mother lives in Baltimore now with her new family. But Pete—he's always been there for me."

What she'd just said about her haphazard family life took me by surprise. I would never have guessed that Alysse's life was anything but blissful. "Sounds kind of challenging," I said.

Alysse started to deny this, and again I could tell she was considering making light of things as usual, but then she seemed to change her mind and, squeezing her shoulders against the back of her neck, said, "Okay, it kind of is. Pete and I only get to visit our mother in the summers, and it's like she has a whole other life now." She blinked at the toes of her boots. "Pete's been sort of bitter about the way things turned out. He said he doesn't even want to go visit next year. I hope he will." She grew quiet.

I nodded slowly, and kept nodding as the lights flickered around us. The band began to play "Winter Wonderland," and Alysse sat up a little and began humming along, her skin glowing in the subdued light, her thick eyelashes casting shadows on her cheeks. In her festive red dress—which to my relief had turned out to have enough fabric in front and even a fairly good-sized portion in the back—she was even more than beautiful. And when she lifted her hand and unconsciously ran her fingers slowly down the side of her elegant neck, I figured it was a good thing I knew who I was and where I was going because I could see how this hormone thing really could mess a guy up if he wasn't thinking ahead.

It was far more than the way her skin glowed, however, and how she looked in her dress or even her sweet smell that was getting to me. It was the closeness I was feeling to her in other ways. She had shed her mask now and then before, but never to this extent. As I looked around the gym, I doubted that many there knew about some of her challenges, and I felt honored that she'd felt she could confide in me.

Apparently nervous that she was talking about herself too much, Alysse pulled herself even farther up with a rustle and a smile. "Okay, enough about boring little me. Now it's your turn, buster. Tell me about *your* family. You say you have a sister getting married?"

"I have two sisters. And yeah, my sister who's just older than me, Monica, is getting married during the Christmas holidays and I'm kind of bummed about it."

Alysse lifted her eyebrows but smiled gently once again. "Why are you bummed about it?"

"She didn't even bother to get *my* permission. One minute she's complaining about always being stuck with this Rulon guy, her roommate's brother. Then, at the end of this last summer, as soon as she gets back to school in Utah, she calls and just like that tells us they're in love and they're getting married and he's the greatest guy who was ever created. Okay, I guess they e-mailed all summer, and it wasn't as if they didn't know each other from the year before. But did she even hint to me or any of us that this was coming? Nooooo."

I was only partly kidding. I *had* felt a little betrayed when Monica had let us know she was getting married. She'd told me all along that she was going on a mission, and we had planned to put in our papers together and leave around the same time, a real brother-sister act, she'd called it. But it hadn't taken me long to adjust—maybe a couple of minutes. How could any of us be anything but happy for her when she was obviously so beyond elated herself? "I just hope this Rulon guy is good enough for her," I added. "My sister's a rock."

"So it sounds like you're the youngest in your family." Alysse removed a piece of tinsel that was falling from her hair, and then another, her eyes still Velcroed to my face.

"Yeah, I'm the youngest." I helped her unknot a stuck piece of tinsel, pulling out tiny strands of dark, silky hair from the loose front part of her hairstyle as I told her about Lynette, my happy-yappy social sibling, and "the big Kipper," as they'd called my brother in high school. I let her know that Lynette and Kip had each made a good match as well and told her about their stellar little families. I told her how we were close—in Kip's case, closer than ever before.

"Brothers and sisters really can be our closest friends and allies, can't they?" Alysse said, more to the silver and white snowflakes glimmering from the ceiling than to me.

"And our toughest critics." I'd finally gotten the tinsel out and I handed it to her and patted down her hair, then carefully brushed back one last small curl.

"Or advisers," she added, stroking the tinsel with her delicate fingers. "My brother's given me some really good advice through the years."

"Yeah, to be more careful, right?"

She laughed softly. "That too."

"My brother always told me the opposite," I admitted. "To loosen up and get a life."

Alysse chuckled again, moved her eyes from the tinsel, and smiled at me reflectively. We sat quietly once more, and as we listened to the medley that had now turned into "Silver Bells," I wondered if I dared mention something I was still really curious about—that I really really wanted to know. Finally I took the plunge. "So, I notice Ren Jensen isn't here tonight. I'm thinking there were a lot of surprised people when you came with me instead of him. The word in Hollenda halls has been that you two are a couple." There, I'd said it.

"*The* couple to watch?" She moved back a little and lifted one shoulder with some apparent discomfort. "You can't believe everything you read in a school paper."

Alysse could probably tell I wanted to know more. "It amazes me how eager people at Hollenda are to match everybody up. Well, I just don't move that fast. I want to take my time when it comes to *couple* kinds of decisions, and I'm not sure I'm ready to be exclusive." She stretched her neck a little. "It's mostly me, but I have some trust issues."

I wanted to say, *Yeah, well, with Ren, it just might be good to have a trust issue.* Instead I tried to be clever. "So are you saying you may be trying to give Ren the . . . umm . . ." I lifted her hem a couple of inches.

"The boot?" She tilted her head again.

I nodded a little too eagerly.

"I'm not sure that I'm giving anyone the boot, but I'm thinking that going to this dance with you may help get a message out there."

Was that the only reason she had asked me? I really wanted to know, but I recognized that it probably shouldn't matter. "Glad I could be of service," I said instead.

"You really do remind me of my brother," Alysse said almost tenderly then. A corner of her mouth was twitching upward. And as she looked at me with those deep blue-green eyes, framed by dark lashes, from a face so right out there, my heart without warning started clip-clopping faster than Tyrone could even think about dancing. Okay, this was not good. I took a deep breath. This was exactly the kind of thing I knew I needed to watch out for. *Tone it down, buckaroo.* Anyway, she'd just told me I reminded her of her brother. And then, as if some guardian angel assigned to make sure I got out there on my mission was tapping the band leader on the shoulder, he announced that the next dance would be the last. Was it really that late? I jerked forward. "What time is it?"

"Eleven-fifty." Allyson was looking at the clock above where the basketball hoop had been folded away.

"That late already?" I followed her eyes to the clock. I'd forgotten about time altogether. *Oh, maaan.* I moved forward in my chair nervously and looked over the dance floor to see if I could spot the people from our group. My father had miraculously extended my curfew at the last minute, but only by a measly fifteen minutes. I was going to have to tell Alysse that if I didn't get home in just over half an hour, I'd be pumpkin meat.

Alysse beat me to it. "Hey, if the whole group of us are Mormons tonight, we probably better get home early, right?"

"I'm afraid so," I said gratefully, melancholy mixed in with relief.

"Time soars when you're having a funtastic time," Alysse said, flashing another gentle, even vulnerable smile in my direction. "And it's been *more* than fun." She touched the back of my hand with the tip of her index finger again and let it linger there for a few seconds. Oh wow. It's the little things.

But by the time I found the presence of mind to open my mouth to agree, Allyson had completely transformed. She was a zany clown again and had started yodeling "Whooo hooo hooo, over here!" to Dansco and Tallulah. "Okay, they're not hearing me!" she said. Before I could respond, she got the attention of a sophomore boy with bright yellow hair. The next thing I knew, this sophomore, Joe, and I were lifting Alysse in her chair and she was swinging my jacket around to get everybody in our group over while happily displaying her green boots. "You okay?" I asked the sophomore.

"Yeah, she's a lot lighter than she acts," he said.

☺

That night, even two or three hours after the dance, I was still on a high. The first date of my life had been one sweet experience.

Funtastic, oh yeah. It'd been more than funtastic. Words were too small to describe what a good time I'd had. In tune with my good mood, Lucky Duck kept barking and batting his tail against the nightstand happily.

"It was good, old boy, yeah, it was good. What a night! Oooooh, yeah! Maaaan. Yes, what a night!" And it was true that it couldn't have been a better evening if I'd special ordered and custom designed it.

My gosh, I'd even been given the chance to share a little information here and there about the gospel in a non-pressured, comfortable way. But after I'd said my prayers and reviewed everything, my good mood gradually dimmed as I recognized that there were so many more things I could have said. I'd been wanting to tell Alysse the real name of the Church, for instance, and I could think of a couple of times during the dance when it would have been easy to do that. In fact, with all the kidding about everybody in our group being Mormon, I could easily have asked her what she *really* knew about the LDS faith. I felt like I could also have expressed support for her decision not to "couple up." Why hadn't I done that? That could have been important. I could have even grabbed a few *For the Strength of Youth* booklets and passed them out. I'd read in the *New Era* about someone who took them everywhere she went. If I'd had any Paul or Alma the Younger in me, I would have done things far differently. Hey, I would have had the whole group converted by the end of the evening, or at least moving in that direction! Wasn't it important to me that Alysse, especially, learned more? *Man*, I remember thinking as I pushed my bottom teeth forward. Why wasn't I more missionary-minded?

But then, after mentally kicking myself for a good half hour, I finally decided to give Kendall Archer a break. This had, after all, been my first date and my first dance. And hey, considering that I'd started off the evening not even being able to operate my tongue, things had turned out amazingly well. Right at the beginning I'd been in too much of a state of panic to share anything, and on the way home I'd been too concerned about making it home on time to think about sharing the gospel. And okay, mid-evening, I'd been caught up in just Alysse. Gradually, as I lay in the dark, I became optimistic again. It wasn't as if there wouldn't be other chances. Alysse and I were far closer now, and it would be easier and more comfortable in the future to move ahead with discussions of that type. Things were also looking good with all my new friends. Oh yeah, there'd be a lot of opportunities to talk to them more.

Chapter Fifteen

I wasn't sure if it was because Allyson had talked to them about me or if it was because they'd seen me in the skit, but during lunch on Monday, Tallulah and Tyrone and some school "thespian" types invited me to join them that following night to watch *Bye Bye Birdie* on DVD. It was a more recent version than the one I'd practically memorized, they let me know, and starred Jason Alexander and Vanessa Williams. "It follows the play script better," Tallulah said.

I invited along Parry, who had expressed an interest in the play earlier but, I was guessing by the way he kept looking at her and elbowing me, was even more interested in Tallulah's long, lean friend, Tanny Willespie.

Arnold, who was no doubt hoping to see Allyson do her thing again, asked if he could tag along that night as well. But as soon as we got to Tallulah's, she told us that Alysse had had a conflict and wasn't able to make it to the get-together. "She always has a lot going on," Tallulah explained.

"Yeah, I can imagine," I responded, my stomach hollowing out with disappointment. But a person can make up his mind to have a good time, and that was what I did. It wasn't hard, with Arnold and Parry setting the example. At first I was content to stay in the background and let those two shine. It soon became obvious, however, that Alysse had left a message with this group that they were to try to talk *me* into trying out for the play. I convinced them to work on my friends instead and let them know I was scheduled to play in the orchestra. I have to say that the evening ended up being pretty fun, especially toward the end when we put on an impromptu skit we called *The Three Scrooges*. My shirt expanded a few sizes when Tallulah laughed and said, "Alysse was right. You really are a funny guy."

On the way home, as Parry and Arnold talked nonstop about the play, I wondered if maybe I could talk to Mr. Hammond about the possibility of my squeezing in a small stage part. Even when I got home I found myself putting off getting to the books as I daydreamed about playing Conrad Birdie, the Elvis-type character in the show. I even went to the mirror and did the old hair-combing thing, my hips at an angle. "Hey, baby," I murmured to Alysse, whom I envisioned in a fifties felt skirt, her ponytail flipping as she swooned and fainted at my presence.

I pulled back, popped my lips, looked down at the dog, and said, "Homework time!" And yeah, it sure was. It was way past homework time and I had to stay up till after eleven and then get up even earlier than usual for seminary to complete my physics and English.

I was still finishing my English during the announcement portion of first period the following morning. Now I understood why Alysse always worked so hard and fast in class when she didn't think anyone was noticing.

It's amazing what can happen to a guy when a popular girl asks him to a dance.

That following weekend I was invited to *three* holiday parties. This time Alysse was at two of them, but so were several other girls who suddenly seemed to want to get to know me. Ren and Nate showed up at Dee Dee's party but left within five minutes, possibly because she was serving cupcakes and punch—not their style of refreshments. I did see Ren talking to Alysse at one point and found it encouraging that neither of them were smiling. After Ren left, Alysse came toward me from the side and pretended to bump into me. Her face was flushed.

She was pulled away almost as quickly as she'd come, but later she came up beside me and socked me softly in the upper arm, which was enough to make my entire weekend.

That following Monday, I found myself in a place I had never in my life imagined I would be sitting: on the central stairs, with people I never thought I'd be sitting by. Arnold couldn't handle it and disappeared quickly. It didn't end there. Less than fifteen minutes later, in homeroom, I was stunned when McKinley, smiling on the screen above us, announced me as one of the finalists for the first semester's Spirit of Hollenda award. "An honor," he read, "extended to the well-rounded, friendly student who most exemplifies the values of the school." Me, well-rounded? I hadn't even made a team. Those around me in my English class didn't seem to think that was a drawback, however. It was nice of them to clap. A couple even cheered.

That Tuesday morning Mrs./Sister Carruber caught me near the front office when I came to check in late after a dental appointment. With tears at the corners of her crinkled eyes, she said quietly, "I just wanted you to know, Kendall, how happy I am that students at Hollenda are recognizing someone with integrity and high standards."

I nodded agreeably until I realized she was talking about *me*. "Oh . . . oh, thanks." I was surprised that I'd been nominated, but again, it wasn't as if I'd won anything.

"Too often the students choose to honor and even follow people who don't have the good moral values and the high academic standards that this award is meant to inspire," she continued. "So when I heard you were on the list, I went home and said to my husband, 'Well, there is justice, after all. A really fine boy has been nominated for something.'" Her voice was warbling with feeling.

The only reason people have been noticing me lately, I felt like saying, *is because Allyson Pringle pays attention to me. That's it.* I didn't say that, however. I just kept my head down, smiled, and mumbled, "Well, thanks, Sister . . . I mean *Mrs.* Carruber, I appreciate that."

But Sister/Mrs. Carruber wasn't finished. She sniffed and,

looking around, said even more quietly, "Maybe you'd better not repeat this little conversation. I wouldn't want to be accused of favoritism."

"Okay," I told her. "I understand."

A few minutes later, Patrice Walters, who also did some tutoring, called to me across the hall. "Hey, Kenny, wanna hang out with a group of us tonight? We're meeting at my house around eight."

Kenny? I was Kenny at school now? I'd thought I was Kenny just to my mom and sisters and, okay, once in a while to Alysse when she was teasing. I wasn't sure I wanted to be Kenny to Patrice Walters.

"I really can't tonight," I called back. "I've got a freight load of homework." I also needed to help Dad with a problem at the warehouse, and I'd told Juan Phineas, the kid I tutored during lunch twice a week, that I would call him. We'd made a breakthrough in math and it was always a good feeling when somebody's eyes lit up with that "Oh, I get it" look. I planned to reinforce what he'd learned with one more problem, just to solidify it.

"Oh, come on," said Patrice. "Homework?"

I lifted my hand. "Yeah, the big *H* word. Seriously, don't tempt me."

It wasn't easy to turn down fun, even when offered by someone who called me Kenny, but I had come to the point where I was dealing with an emergency. If I didn't come up with a decent science project, I could kiss away even a B-plus in physics. You can get behind fast, and my A had already done a vanishing act. This social stuff was new to me, and I was finding out that being in demand had its challenges. I admired Alysse for fitting as much into her life as she did. No wonder she didn't waste time.

"I'm locking myself downstairs," I told my mother as soon as I whooshed into the kitchen along with a gust of snow and wind. Mom was apparently taking a little break from the sewing room and was sitting at the kitchen table earnestly folding together what looked like some kind of fabric flowers.

"Well, it looks like you have plenty of research material," she said, making an effort to smile over her glasses. She was right, I did have plenty of material. I'd talked Arnold into swinging by the Kalamazoo City Library with me on the way home, and I also planned to get right to the computer as soon as I got downstairs. I'd begged off going to the warehouse.

Mom broke off a piece of thread with her teeth. "You want to talk about your project? I can listen while I sew these together."

"That's okay." We'd batted ideas back and forth before, but it was pretty obvious, by the way her lips remained stretched across her teeth even after she'd bitten off the thread, that she was stressed to the hilt with wedding stuff. Dad had picked up on her tension a few days before and had mentioned that he was worried about Mom's blood pressure. He'd been trying to talk Mom into taking a break and going with him for a few days on a business trip to New York.

I hoped she would. I was worried myself about how she'd been groaning loudly the last few days and banging things around in the sewing room. "You can help me by not answering the phone," I said, reaching down to pat Lucky Duck, who was licking the snow off my boots.

"Well, you have been getting a lot more phone calls lately," my mother said.

"You might say I've been discovered," I told her. She watched me pull off my boots, which I had realized were tracking in mud.

"Well, I can see why. I'm glad you're having fun."

"Only I've been having a little *too* much fun lately. In fact, I'll leave this upstairs." I reached into my backpack and slid my phone across the table. "I need to work without interruption. It's an emergency."

⊚

Anticipating a late night, I'd finished my Spanish during lunch and started my English homework on the way to the library. Within seconds after I got downstairs, I was working on the physics assignment that was due the following day so that I could devote a couple of hours to my science project. At least I had finally come up with an idea.

I gave Juan a call after I finished my basic homework, then rushed up to dinner—the straight-from-the-freezer kind again. The freezer thing was fine with me, I let Mom know—faster than takeout. And I hurried down as soon as I'd stuffed in the last potato "dollop." This time I got so involved in my project plans and outline that I kept my focus for a good three hours. By ten o'clock I was stretching with satisfaction, feeling fairly good about the progress I'd made. There was still a lot to do, but I'd gotten a good, solid start and it had been a productive afternoon. Lucky could sense my satisfaction and again beat his tail happily against the floor.

After family prayer, all I had time to do was to finish my English. I'd dedicated so much time to my project, there was no time for history, and I hadn't so much as glanced at my textbook or notes for several days, but I really wasn't worried. I had accurately predicted Thorndike's previous three "pop" tests. As I pulled my pillow up over my face around eleven, I remember thinking: *What if Mr. Thorndike pulls a fast one tomorrow?* I quickly assured myself that it wouldn't happen. It was far too soon for another test. We hadn't covered nearly enough material. No, there was no way.

Chapter Sixteen

S tudents, remove all books and papers from your desks please," said Mr. Thorndike at the beginning of history that next day.

"A test," someone at the far side of the room moaned.

"That's right," said Mr. Thorndike. "I'm assuming that those of you who are complaining haven't kept current on the material like I warned you to do. I believe I told you about the importance of reviewing the chapters and class notes daily. If you don't learn that in high school you'll have a rude awakening in college." It was something we'd heard before, like maybe five dozen times.

Shooooot. Without looking around, not even at Allyson, I shut my eyes and gritted my teeth. I'd been so sure Mr. Thorndike would wait until we finished a few more sections of the chapter that I hadn't even done a once-over of the material.

Some kids are bright enough to wing tests. I just didn't

happen to be one of them. In other words, my good grades have always been a result of hard work, not amazing brainpower.

I lowered my head to my desk, my temples throbbing. This was bad. I'd be getting my lowest grade ever. I figured there was a good chance I'd even flunk this test—a first for me. Why had I let myself get so carried away this past week with all the social stuff? I was pretty miffed at myself and felt I should have known this would happen. Good-bye, scholarship. My head lowered, I pressed my fist against my forehead, then lifted my eyes to watch Mr. Thorndike count out the tests for our row with what I was sure was a self-satisfied look on his face.

After a copy of the test reached me, I left it on the desk face-down for a good ten to fifteen seconds. Finally, I reluctantly flipped over the familiar off-white sheet with blue lines and looked at question number one. "Who was elected president in 1856?" It was a simple, straightforward question. Unfortunately, I didn't know the answer. Not a good start. I could name the first four or five U.S. presidents, but we were talking eighty years after George Washington. In fact, Thomas Jefferson and John Adams had died about thirty years before that, on the same year and the same day: July 4th. I'd read that once in one of those little-known history facts books; it was the kind of thing you remember, but I doubted it would be on the test. I tapped my pencil.

The only president I could think of who would have been living around about that time was good old "Honest" Abe, who not only saved our country but filed important papers in his top hat—another one of those useless facts I'd once read. I filled in his name, took a deep breath, and moved on to question number two, a true/false: "Abraham Lincoln defeated Stephen Douglas in the senate race of 1858." Okay, so much for Abraham Lincoln being president in 1856. I erased his name and exhaled slowly before I went to the next question.

"In the _____ _____ case, the Supreme Court ruled that slaves were only property," question number three read. I didn't have the slightest idea what belonged in the blanks. I moved to four, then five. I thought I knew the answer to question number six, but again wasn't sure about seven. By the end of the test I'd left three-quarters of the answers blank. It was time to start guessing, especially on the true/false, where I'd at least have a fifty-fifty chance. But there were only six true/false questions. "And now," said Mr. Thorndike, clicking his stopwatch, "you have precisely thirty seconds to finish your test. When I say *stop*, you will immediately lay down your pencils." I hurriedly began filling in the true/false. Figuring the odds would be with me if I filled in all one or the other, I decided on *true* and wrote the word out six times. Thorndike didn't like us to just put a *T* or an *F* because it was too easy to get them mixed up. I'd swirled my last *e* when Mr. Thorndike belted out, "STOP!" After we'd all placed our pencils on our desks, he asked us to pass forward our tests. I reluctantly relinquished mine, then leaned my face in my folded hands. There had been only seven or eight answers I'd been fairly sure about—mostly review questions—and that was it. To add to my humiliation, Mr. Thorndike let us know that we would be correcting one another's tests immediately. Grinding my molars, I blinked slowly and pulled myself up, but not very straight, as I wondered who would get my test and think I was a first-rate dunce. It was at this point I glanced at Allyson, who wagged her eyebrows at me twice, pretending as usual not to have a care in the world.

Carefully flipping through the tests, Mr. Thorndike was taking the usual pains to make sure that none of us would end up correcting our own. Kerrie Masanto's test came to me. Kerrie was possibly the most studious girl in our entire grade, and I knew if she hadn't done well probably nobody else had either. A second later I marked her first answer correct. It was James Buchanan who was elected president in 1856. Kerrie got number two right as well. I'd guessed correctly on that one myself. It was a pretty well-known fact that Abe Lincoln didn't win much of anything until he won president.

I'm sorry to say that when Mr. Thorndike read the answer to number three, the *Dred Scott* case, and Kerrie missed it, I wasn't all that unhappy about it. And when she missed numbers five and ten as well, I didn't exactly mourn for the girl. By the end of the test, Kerrie, who was generally a hundred-percenter, had missed seven. Out of respect, I'd marked fairly small *X*s on her wrong answers and good-sized *C*s by the correct responses. I knew from experience that there were people in our class who enjoyed making giant *X*s, but I wasn't about to be one of them. In fact, when I saw Kerrie glancing around the room, she looked so much like one of those little cartoon hound dogs that I felt compassion for the girl, and actually found myself wishing I could turn some of her *X*s to *C*s. Missing seven was uncharacteristic for the girl with the thick glasses and heavy braces, and I figured she was feeling about as lousy as I was. And I *was* feeling lousy. The gamble I'd taken by filling *trues* into all the true/false slots had backfired. All but one of the answers was false. No, it wasn't my lucky day.

"Now, if you'll please pass the tests you just corrected forward," said Mr. Thorndike, "I'll record these tonight and get them back to you tomorrow."

Can't wait, I thought.

For the rest of the class period I kept my head low as I tried to figure out how much this one test would cost me. I really needed a scholarship if I wanted to go to school in Utah. Now that my physics grade had slipped, I'd been counting on at least an A-minus in history. I was pretty upset with myself for not using my time more wisely and felt I could have done a far better balancing act. I would need to get almost perfect scores on the remaining test and the final in order to keep my grade point up in the high Bs. I pulled myself up in my seat and vowed there'd be no more second-guessing this teacher with the bifocals, scowl, and bouncing bow tie. I should have remembered how much Thorndike enjoyed keeping people guessing. I pictured him saying to his wife later that night (with satisfaction in his tone), "There were quite a few surprised students when I announced we were having a test today, dear." No, I should have known Thorndike would do his best to catch us off guard.

By the end of the class period, however, I'd decided that it was counterproductive to kick myself too hard. I just needed to "gird up my loins," a scripture term that my brother always made fun of during our family's attempts at scripture study time, but that I personally kind of liked. In fact, I decided that that was exactly what I'd do: I'd gird up my courage and motivation and move on. No more social stuff on weeknights; I'd limit that to weekends and keep it down even at that. After class I pulled out my assignment book and made a lengthy list of things I needed to do that week.

I didn't have a tutoring appointment that day, so I had hitched a ride with Arnold. While he drove home, happily talking nonstop about the Australian outback to another friend, Beezer, who'd also needed a ride, I reviewed the headings of the upcoming sections of the history chapter, skimming through everything quickly.

The kitchen was empty when I got home, and a note on the fridge let me know Mom had gone to get more lace. It was just as well. I had my action plan ready, and without even stopping for a snack I headed for the computer/sewing room, where I quickly caught up some business entries so I could get to history pronto. By the time Mom walked in, I was at the desk in my room and had already finished reviewing five sections of chapter fourteen in my history book—"The Post Civil War Era."

"Looks like you're going at it again, huh?"

"Yeah," I grunted. Then I looked up with a smile. "And so are you."

She nodded but hung around. "Dad's still trying to talk me into going with him on his business trip to New York, and Lynette's trying to convince me to go too. There's a seamstress in her ward who she thinks can help get things finished up."

I looked up and smiled. "Go for it! Seriously."

"Kenny, I can't. We're just a few days away from the wedding."

"I'll bet it'll be just fine. You say Lynette has a seamstress she could line up?"

"What if that didn't work out? And you'd be here alone."

"Mom." I gave her one of my looks.

"Well, it's still too risky and close to the wedding." She patted my shoulder and then headed down the hall.

As soon as I heard her machine going again, I started on an outline for my English term paper. I was so used to the background whirring of the sewing machine by now, it was almost as if I relied on it. After finishing the paper and sticking it in my folder, I went back to history and reviewed again what I'd just reviewed. Then I pulled my science project stuff from the top of my chest of drawers. It wasn't until time for family prayer that I went upstairs and checked my messages. There were three more invitations for me to hang out.

The next day in Spanish, Alysse asked in a fairly casual tone, "So, how'd you do on yesterday's history test?"

It wasn't really something I was anxious to talk about. "Umm, not so good."

"*How* not so good?"

"About as not so good as a person can do," I admitted unhappily. "I was thinking we had at least another two or three days, maybe even a week before Thorndike pulled another test on us. I guess he's trying to squeeze in as much as possible before the holiday break. How about you? How'd you do?"

"I passed by about this much," Alysse held her thumb and index finger a pencil-width portion apart. "Actually, make it this much," she said, bringing them even closer together. "I had an advantage, though. I heard through the grapevine that Thorndike might be planning another test, and I had a chance to thumb through the chapter really fast."

"Well, I guess I'm not a part of that network," I said a little bitterly.

"I should have let you know. Sorry," said Alysse. "But hey, you never know. Be an optimist! I predict you did way better than you think you did." Her overly cheerful tone should probably have sent little flashing signals my way.

Instead I huffed out a scornful laugh of disagreement, mumbled, "yeah, right," and thought nothing more about her comment or even the fact that she again wiggled her eyebrows up and down three instead of only two times in a row.

Chapter Seventeen

I should have caught on for sure that something was going on when, in sixth period, Alysse and those around her—Jake and Molly, for instance—kept glancing my way as Mr. Thorndike passed back our tests.

"Not your generally perfect score," I heard Thorndike say to a mortified Kerrie. I didn't have much time to feel sorry for her because he was moving toward my side of the room. I readjusted myself in my seat, wondering what clever comment he would make to *me* when he handed me my grade. Instead, without a word, he handed Jen Fern hers. I caught a quick glance at a minus eighteen just before Jen rammed the sheet into her folder.

When Mr. Thorndike flipped me my test, I laid it facedown on my desk, thinking maybe I'd just avoid turning it over for, say, the rest of my life. But then Mr. Thorndike threw me a curve. "Congratulations, Kendall, you got the high in the class. Twenty-nine out of thirty correct."

My eyebrows knotted together, I stared at the bald spot on the back of Thorndike's head as he walked away, then lifted the top corner of my test. Sure enough, there in large, bold, even underlined print was the number 29. Impossible. "Excuse me, Mr. Thorndike," I said, raising a couple of fingers, "but this can't be my test."

"What do you mean?" Thorndike took the few steps back to me, his normally sour expression even more surly. Adjusting his glasses, he took the test paper from me. But then he smiled in that kind of prunelike way of his. "I was under the impression your name was Kendall Archer. Isn't that still your name?"

"Yeah . . . but . . ."

"Well, as far as I know there are no other Kendall Archers in this class or in any of my other classes." He pointed to the lefthand corner of the paper at what was sure enough my name in what appeared to be my handwriting. "Here you go." With that, he patted the test back down on my desk and walked away, smirking at his cleverness.

As Mr. Thorndike continued returning the exams, my eyes scanned the test. It was my name at the top all right, exactly as I had written it, but that was just about all that looked the same. The spaces I'd left blank were no longer blank. Even the incorrect answers had been crossed through and correct responses scribbled neatly and boldly in handwriting very similar to mine, but not mine. I glanced around the room until it struck me where I should be looking. Sure enough, those sitting around Alysse were full-blown grinning in my direction. Alysse had her head down and her lips tucked in at the corners.

Without smiling I turned forward and blinked, leaving my lids lowered for an extra second as I recognized what I should have immediately guessed. In slow motion, I pulled out my binder, my mind racing. *Okay, now what do I do?* The grades would already be recorded in Mr. Thorndike's computer, including this *A* I hadn't even come close to earning. On the other hand, there was nothing Mr. Thorndike would relish more than to have something on the girl who even now was wearing a headband of bells. I opened my lips slightly and blew out the air I'd been holding in.

After class I didn't move from my seat for several seconds as I continued trying to decide what to do. Under normal circumstances there would have been no hesitation whatsoever. But now, leaving the test sheet in my folder, I rose slowly, then placed one foot in front of the other until I found myself out in the hall.

The light from the adjacent window hit my face with a wallop, but when my eyes adjusted, I saw that Alysse had already been whisked away by her friends on the drill team. She grinned at me from well down the hall, motioning me to join them.

I raised my palm in response, and, since the sun was still in my eyes, might have looked like I was smiling. But I wasn't smiling. "Hey, Kenny!" It was Patrice again. "You heading to AB hall? I'll walk with you!"

"No, I'm heading to the main hall," I said, not sounding all that sorry about it. "Catch you next time."

"*Kenny* here just got the high on the history test," Molly teased, swinging her black and white bag. "Sorry, Patrice, he probably thinks he's too smart for everybody now. Right, Kenny?"

I huffed out a sound of some kind, something between a grunt and a sigh.

After school, Arnold, who'd been stuck like melted wax on the fact that a friend of his had actually been nominated for the Spirit of Hollenda award, mentioned it for about the trillionth time. "You don't look very happy for someone who could easily be voted Mr. Spirit of Hollenda soon," he said, out of breath as usual. "What's wrong, mate? I'd be kicking my heels together if I were you."

"Alysse has really done it this time," I said, craning my neck as I looked around. Even though Lexie wasn't at her locker yet, the girl could sneak up on you.

"What's she done this time?" Arnold lifted his upper lip and got ready to snicker. When he saw that I wasn't looking even a little amused, his smile faded.

"Remember how I told you I flunked the surprise test in Thorndike's class yesterday?" I asked him quietly.

"I remember you said something about flunking something, but you're always saying stuff like that."

"Well, this time I know for sure I flunked the test because I left a big bunch blank and then I hardly got any right that I guessed on."

"Been there, done that," said Arnold, sounding unimpressed.

"So now take a look." I leaned my backpack against my locker door, pulled the test from the folder, and handed it to Arnold, who looked up in confusion.

"I thought you just said you left a whole bunch blank."

"I did."

"Then I don't get it. How . . ." Arnold's mouth rounded into a small circle and he looked back down at the test, then up again. "Uh-oh. Allyson corrected this?"

I nodded with lowered lids. "I don't know how she managed to get my test, but somehow she did."

Arnold filled his cheeks up with air and let it out in one large guffaw.

"It's not funny."

"Sorry, mate," he said. "I didn't mean to do that. I can see why you don't think it's funny, but it's just that it's so like something Alysse would do. You know, outrageous." He stuffed the test into my backpack pocket.

"Yeah, it's vintage Allyson all right," I said, relocating the test to the inside side pocket with some of my other tests. "Except what am I supposed to do now? I can't accept an *A* on a test I flunked." I swung the backpack around.

Throwing *his* huge yellow bag, which looked like it had half the county in it, over his shoulder, Arnold said, "Hack into Thorndike's web site and change the grade?"

"Yeah, right."

"I'm kidding."

"I know." My friend often said *I'm kidding* when he didn't need to.

Carefully studying my face, he asked then, "You're not thinking about turning in Alysse, I hope? Because you really can't do that. You get Allyson Pringle in trouble and the whole school will be down on you. The yell leaders would be doing a cheer that goes something like 'Kick Kendall Archer! Kick Kendall Archer! Karate chop! Karate chop! Kick Kendall Archer!'" Arnold's bag slid from his arm and he had to catch it with one hand as he swung the other arm with full impact, his light red hair flying straight up as he did. It wasn't a bad impression of a one-armed yell leader, and I couldn't help laughing a little. But then my cheeks tightened across my cheekbones.

"Of course I don't want to get Allyson in trouble. I'd probably be doing a cheer like that myself about somebody who fouled up Alysse. She's a good friend and I'd never want to do anything that would mess her up. That's what's making this so hard to figure out."

Fully expecting Arnold to make some crack again about Alysse being even more to me than just a good friend, I readjusted my backpack, slammed my locker shut, checked the lock, and leaned down to pick up my trombone case. *Don't say it*, I willed him silently. I really, really didn't want him to say the words I was afraid might be true.

I'd spotted Lexie and Bernard and several others at the end of the hall at this point, and I pulled Arnold in the direction of the stairs. "Here's the problem," I said soberly. "A couple of months ago I would never have guessed so many people knew I was a member of the Church. In fact, I thought nobody even knew who I was, period. But I found out this semester that people do seem to know, for whatever reason. And if they didn't know it before, they do now that Alysse has been sailing it out there like a flag."

I'd already told Arnold about my group at the dance all "acting Mormon," or at least thinking they were acting Mormon.

"*And* now that you're getting nominated for everything," Arnold interrupted. "Don't forget that."

"Everything? I was nominated for one thing." I shook my head at his exaggeration. "Hey, believe me, Arn, they know you're LDS, too."

"I tell everybody," said Arnold. He had a point. Arnold was always happy to share the gospel, even with those who didn't particularly want to hear it. "But where are you heading with this?" Arnold lifted his hand and called out a hello to Ross somebody and Millie, a buddy of Dora's, who were on their way down the stairs. They raised their hands back.

"And hi, JJ and J," Millie called, practically singing the words, her large eyes blinking.

"Hi there," I said, lifting my chin. I watched the girls reach the top, then returned my attention to Arnold.

"Okay, my point is, even if I didn't mind being dishonest personally—and it happens that I really do—having people think Mormons cheat wouldn't do much for the Church or the missionary effort, now, would it? We're a small minority here at Hollenda. We're the only representatives: you, me, your sisters, and Sist—I mean *Mrs.* Carru. Basically we're it in the school."

Arnold shrugged and nodded. "Okay, that could be true. We're the Church at Hollenda. You and me and Ella and Bella and Mrs. Carru. But look at it this way: Having everybody in the school hate you because you got their favorite person in trouble wouldn't help the Church's image much either, now, would it?"

What he'd just said made sense, and I plodded along next to him with heavy feet.

As we headed into the heavier traffic near the front hall, Arnold got caught a few people behind me. He screeched to a halt so he wouldn't run into a girl carrying what looked like a couple of cardboard smokestacks, excused himself cheerfully, and, lifting his arms, caught up with me again. "I say you'd definitely better just forget it and accept that A. Besides, there's the award you're up for. No way will you win if you turn in Alysse."

In an effort to avoid the stairs, I turned quickly and led him out the side door, where I pulled to a stop because this was getting ironic now. "So, what you're saying is I'd have a better chance at winning a values award if I accepted a grade I didn't earn?" I puffed out my cheeks. "Something's wrong with that picture."

"Okay, okay, you're right, that doesn't make a whole lot of sense." Arnold raised his free arm. "Hey, I don't claim to have all the answers. But sometimes there isn't a good choice, if you know what I mean. Sometimes you just gotta do what you gotta do and move on. I say in this case you've gotta forget it."

I sighed because my good friend was completely right about the part that there didn't seem to be any good choices here. "Hey!" Dee Dee had spotted me, and Caleb raised his hand as well. "Are you coming to the stairs, my bro?"

"Save me a seat for tomorrow. I need to head out."

What I really needed was to think.

Chapter Eighteen

Dad had miraculously succeeded in convincing Mom to go to New York with him and it was quiet at our house—just me and the dog.

The phone rang several times, but I ignored it as I paced from the kitchen to the living room, downstairs to the computer room, and back upstairs again, Lucky Duck right at my heels as ever. Maybe I felt that if I paced long enough and thought hard enough I'd come up with a solution. There had to be one. Wasn't there always a solution? Well, if there was, I sure wasn't thinking of it, and I plopped down on a kitchen chair and put my head on the table. As I half sat, half lay there, rehashing everything, I actually began to believe that my quirky friend Arnold, who liked to fake an Australian accent and had recently bought himself an outback hat, just might be right.

Regardless of what was the honest or right thing to do, regardless of how wrong it felt to accept a grade I didn't earn, I couldn't risk getting Alysse into trouble with Thorndike and the school. Not only was she much more vulnerable than anyone would ever have guessed but, despite what certain teachers were convinced of, she was a fantastic human being. Sure, too often she stepped over the zaniness line, but the good she did far outweighed the crazy, impulsive things she also did. Thorndike didn't know what she was really like. Filling in the answers on my test had been wrong, yes, but from her viewpoint it had just been a big joke, and possibly even a not-too-well-thought-out favor for a good friend. Well, Thorndike wouldn't interpret it as a joke. I knew this teacher would interpret what Alysse had done as some kind of a criminal act. Oh, how I wished she didn't act so over the top sometimes. Why did she feel so compelled to do that?

Then I thought about how this same zaniness drew people out. I thought about what she'd done for Charlotte, for instance, who looked healthier than I'd ever seen her in the months since she'd been crowned homecoming attendant. I thought about all Alysse had done for *me* and what a good time we'd had all year and the amazing time we'd had at that dance that I would remember forever.

Ever since the dance Alysse had even made it a point to say hi to Arnold and joke around with him a little, which thrilled him, of course. No wonder he didn't want me to turn her in. How many other kids at our school felt lifted up because of her? Besides, hadn't Christ told us not to throw the first stone at someone who'd made a mistake? Getting Alysse in trouble would be like throwing that stone. People came first, didn't they?

I really started rationalizing then. This was, after all, one little test we were talking about, almost a quiz. What did it matter? Everybody cheated. The last time Mrs. Cavanaugh had left the room during an exam, half the kids in English had whipped out their books or compared answers. Kids in our school sneakily text-messaged answers to each other even when teachers were right there in the room. Cheating had become about as commonplace at our school as ordering pizza for lunch. I was making a big deal out of something kids did *constantly.* Anyway, it wasn't as if I'd asked for or had wanted Alysse to do this. I'd had nothing to do with it. I needed to remember that. I also needed to remember that I tended to be way over the top when it came to conscientiousness.

It wasn't until about six o'clock that I finally stopped pacing and sat down at the computer so I could enter some business data I'd promised Dad I would get to. Next I made it back to my room, dragging my backpack behind me. Around seven, I went upstairs to scrounge up something to eat. After I popped a couple of mini pizzas in the microwave, I checked my messages to see who'd called. Along with more people at school who wanted me to hang out—some I didn't even know—my sister Lynette had left a message, asking about the bridesmaid dresses. Mom had asked me to run them over to her so the seamstress in her ward could finish them up. I quickly pushed her number. "Is tomorrow night okay for me to bring over that stuff?"

"That should be fine," Lynette said. "Sister Mackintosh said she wouldn't be starting on them until first thing Saturday anyway. Can you stay for tacos when you come?" Then she added sheepishly, "And do you think we could talk you into tending for a couple of hours?"

Judging by the degree of screeching in the background, I figured Lynette could probably use the break. The Skipper tended to get grumpy at night. Just the same, it soothed me to be around the little guy. And maybe I needed the change of scenery. "Sure, I could do that," I said. I hesitated then, wondering if I should bring up my dilemma and get Lynette's input. But then again, maybe I didn't want her input. Maybe I was afraid she would try to change my mind when I'd pretty much already made my decision. The little guy was really crying now. "Oh, shoot, Skipper just fell off the step stool," Lynette said, and quickly excused herself.

Arnold called as soon as I hung up. He pretended to be calling to see if I could give him a ride to the holiday concert on Saturday night that we were both participating in, but I knew he was really calling to see what I'd decided to do about the situation with Allyson. "You know what, mate," I said, "I've been thinking about that situation with the test and Alysse, and I'm thinking you're probably right that I just need to go ahead and accept that grade."

"Yeah, there's nothing else can you do." He sounded relieved.

After I hung up from talking with Arnold, I opened the fridge to see if there was anything else worth eating in there, but then shut it because for some reason I didn't have much of an appetite—a first for me. I plodded back downstairs, Lucky Duck right behind me again, and pulled open my backpack, then opened my English notebook and began working on alliteration. But I couldn't seem to concentrate. Why didn't I feel better about my decision when I knew full well there just really was no other route? *I won't think about it*, I decided. I closed the notebook, then opened my history textbook and thumbed through our last chapter for the fourth time. Finally I shut the book, exhaled, leaned back in my chair, and stared down the hall. Monica's wedding gown, which Mom had insisted she would finish herself, was hanging on the back of the sewing room door.

It was really hard for me to envision my sister, who could spike a volleyball like nobody I'd ever seen, actually putting on that dress and getting married. But it looked like that was exactly what was going to happen—and soon. She'd called just a couple of days before to find out from Mom what to expect in the temple interview appointment with the bishop, and I'd given her a bad time. "I sure hope you repented of that time you painted the bathroom with magic marker," I teased her.

"Oh, gosh, I totally forgot about that," she played along.

In person I could always tell when she was kidding by the way she held her mouth, but now I wasn't sure. "Hey, not really," I said. "Good grief, you were four or five years old!"

"Gotcha," she laughed. "I'm kidding too. Like I can worry about what I did that long ago."

We'd chuckled about it at the time, but afterwards I had wondered if teasing someone about a temple interview would be considered light-minded. Well, I wasn't laughing now. I'd be going through that same interview myself in not that many months, and then I'd be heading out into the field to teach the gospel of Jesus Christ—the gospel of truth. "So what do I tell the bishop if he asks me if I'm honest in my dealings?" I asked my dog quietly. "Do I say I'm honest except for once in a while when I accept grades I don't deserve?"

Lucky Duck tilted his head and let out a little woof. Not much of an answer. But he was a dog, after all—a really good dog, yeah, but still a dog. So why was I having a heart-to-heart with a dog? I realized then who I should be talking with, and it wasn't my dog.

I slid down from my desk and onto my knees. I really needed confirmation that what I was thinking of doing—or should I say *not doing*—was okay with Him. Basically I needed some peace.

You always hope with prayers that answers will come immediately and be presented to you on a tray the second you finish your prayer. I waited for probably a full five minutes on my knees, then got up and wandered around, seeking insight. If I wasn't going to get my answer on a tray, I wanted at least a side dish or something—anything that let me know that what Arnold had suggested and what I'd decided was the right decision, really was okay. Even a Pop Tart would do.

Finally I went back to my desk and opened my history book again and stared at the next chapter heading: "The Carpetbagger Era." I read the first couple of sentences, then pushed my book aside, leaned back, and grabbed the scriptures off my nightstand for a different kind of history. Within ten minutes I spotted three references to honesty in the Book of Mormon. I sighed, closed my scriptures, replaced them on my nightstand, and went into the bathroom to brush my teeth. As I hit the molars in almost slow motion, I remembered about the stupor of thought the scriptures tell us about—that if an answer is wrong, we draw a blank. I wasn't sure if what I was feeling was a stupor, but it certainly wasn't a pleasant, A-okay feeling. It was more of a draining, heavy, things-are-not-at-all-okay feeling. It was an I'm-a-two-hundred-year-old-man-and-my-feet-weigh-five-hundred-pounds-each feeling.

Mom always accused me of being older and wiser than my age, but I didn't think this was what she was talking about. I decided to go to bed so I could get up earlier than usual and pray again then. Just before I lay down, I remembered my tooth guard and I grabbed it from my stand and adjusted it into my mouth, figuring I'd probably be needing it.

Chapter Nineteen

Brother Aspen was generally understanding when people dozed off in early morning seminary, and it was a lucky thing, because when you don't get to sleep until two-thirty, and you have to get up at five-thirty, it happens. I'd been tired before with all the stuff going on at our house, but this was the worst. It felt kind of like I'd been beaten over the head with an anvil. Nice old guy that he was, Brother Aspen waited until after class to place his wide palm on my shoulder. "You okay, Kip?"

Kip? I didn't bother to correct him. Brother Aspen often joked about having taught seminary since Old Testament times. I wasn't sure how long he'd really been teaching, but it was long enough that he often called us by our siblings' or, in some instances, even our parents' names. "It's not like you to fall asleep during seminary, son," he continued. "Usually you're taking notes and marking scriptures." His eyes were kind.

"Yeah, and I'll need to catch up. I, umm . . ." I decided to explain somewhat. "I just have some things on my mind that I've been losing sleep over."

"Is it something I can help with?"

I watched Arnold walk away from us backwards, almost bumping into a couple of people. "I don't know if anyone can help. It's complicated." I wasn't sure whether to tell him more. Arnold headed out the door, obviously anxious to leave. The classroom had emptied quickly, and I turned back to Brother Aspen. "Okay, what if you have a problem and there doesn't seem to be a clear answer?"

"I imagine you've prayed about it."

"Yes."

My teacher lifted his ample head and brought it down slowly. "I've noticed in my own life that sometimes things that seem complicated really aren't. We make things complicated, but they're not necessarily complicated with God. You just may already know the answer." He lowered himself into the chair next to me. "Have you talked to your Mom or Dad about this, Kip?" Brother Aspen had served with my father as his counselor in the stake Young Men's organization a few years before.

"My sister's getting married in not that many days and the whole family's pretty involved in that," I explained. I didn't tell him that my parents also happened to be in another state and that I wasn't really a spill-out-your-troubles-over-the-phone kind of guy. I wasn't even a share-your-troubles-with-your-seminary-teacher kind of guy. "I'm Kendall and not Kip, by the way."

"Oh, yes, *Kendall*. Sorry. I always do that, don't I? Kendall! Kendall!" I felt bad I'd mentioned anything when he shook his head so hard that his bottom lip flapped. "I'm sorry." He paused and took a breath. "Well, *Kendall*, I'd suggest you start there. You have great parents, and I'll bet they'd make the time to talk with you in spite of everything that's going on. But, in the meantime, do keep praying. It sometimes takes time, but in my experience eventually Heavenly Father opens a door or window and helps us see the solution to a problem."

"Okay, thanks, Brother Aspen." I looked toward the door where Arnold, his hair already starting to fan out, was poking in his head.

Brother Aspen lifted his hand to Arnold, then smiled at me with concern. "You let me know if you want to talk about this any more fully, young man."

"I'll do that." I wondered at this point if it was God's will that I make an appointment with Brother Aspen. Was the old guy right that this might be more black and white than I was guessing? I didn't see how it could be anything but complicated. Sometimes life wasn't black and white.

"What'd he say?" Arnold asked as we hurried to his car.

"That life isn't as complicated as we make it."

"Just what I told you," said my friend.

My fatigue in seminary was nothing compared to how it hit me first period. By third period Spanish there was a giant mushroom in my head.

In contrast, Alysse seemed well rested and as upbeat as usual.

"*Hola,*" she said, her eyes crinkling mischievously from behind her red glasses. She was wearing a furry pair of antlers this time, again reminding everyone that Christmas was just around the corner. "Hey, for somebody who thought he'd flunked the history test, you did pretty well," she teased.

"I sure did," I said without inflection. "Amazing, isn't it, since I didn't study."

Alysse opened her Spanish book without taking her eyes from me. "You don't sound very happy for someone who just got an *A* on a test he didn't even study for."

I hesitated and sighed. "I'm not, Alysse."

"Uh-oh, does Kenny need big hanky again?" I could tell this was another attempt to make me laugh, but Alysse didn't seem to be putting as much into the chipmunk-Elmo role as she had in the past.

"The problem is that I didn't earn that *A*. I mean, I really did fail the thing."

"Oh, boy. Here we go. Well, why am I surprised?" Alysse rolled her eyes and shook her head in what I hoped was mock disgust, the chipmunk voice gone. "So tell me this," she said, picking up a rubber band from the floor and aiming it in my direction. "Have you ever done anything wrong in your life?" The rubber band hit me on the left hand.

"Have I ever done anything wrong?" I smiled sadly. "Hasn't everybody?" I picked up the rubber band very slowly because my whole body felt like it was lifting it. When I started to stretch the elastic, I didn't even have the energy to do that. Or maybe I just wasn't in the mood.

"Let me guess. You've done one, maybe two things wrong in

your life?" Alysse took the elastic from my hand and stretched it around her fist and onto her wrist.

"More like a half dozen." I tried to smile at my joke. "And I wish that were true," I added. I *did* wish that I'd only done a half dozen things wrong in my life. I'd done hundreds of things wrong—maybe not any major kind of things, but a lot of little things that added up when you put them together. And that was why I always felt lucky that I'd been raised with the assurance that when we give it our very best shot, Christ fills in the gaps. But I'd also been taught, and had learned from experience, that it saves you a lot of grief to just make the right decision in the first place rather than to have to fix it later.

"What'd you do, take some gum from your mom's purse when you were three or four? Or did you call somebody in your family a bad name like, umm, *stupid?*"

"Worse than that, I'm afraid." I'd actually taken a ten from the money jar once because I was mad at my mother for handing Kip that amount outright when I was the one who'd cleaned the entire kitchen. It's true that I'd had no intention of keeping that money, and I'd returned it later that night, but I *had* taken it. Then there was the time the Garbett brothers and I played a dirty trick on the poor Crane family down the street. When we hadn't been able to come up with a crane company willing to send a crane, we'd just ordered cabs to their house several times in a row. As if they could even afford cabs. That had felt worse.

"Uh-huh. Maybe you made some prank phone calls, and that's about as bad as it gets," said Alysse.

I was beginning to think she really could read minds.

"Well, you know what?" Her voice took on a serious tone. "I can tell this is going to eat away at you, so why don't you just do what you feel you need to do. I really don't care."

"There's a big problem with that," I said. "It's that there's no way I'm going to foul you up. I refuse to do that."

"Hey, I said I don't care, didn't I? It's my problem, not yours. I know how you operate, and I'm not going to be responsible for you carrying around this burden of guilt for the rest of your life. And besides, what can Thorndike do to me, anyway? I mean seriously, who cares?" She was acting tough, but I knew her well enough to know that she was bluffing—that she *did* care. Talking to Alysse about it hadn't made the situation any easier.

It wasn't until a few minutes later, when Señor Alvarez passed back the Spanish vocab quizzes and I saw the initials R.P. (indicating that Rhonda Pate across the room had corrected my test), that something hit me like a bolt and then moved through me like an electrical surge. I couldn't believe I hadn't thought of it before. I sat up and grinned, fully awake and re-energized. Señor Alvarez and most of my other teachers always had us initial the tests we corrected. For some reason, Mr. Thorndike didn't do that. I'd wondered about that in the past. Oh, once in a while I'd gone ahead and just initialed a history test I corrected out of habit, but for the most part, since our teacher didn't seem to care, I didn't bother or I just forgot. I wasn't sure why Thorndike didn't have us identify ourselves on the tests we corrected. Maybe he'd never had any problems in that regard. Well, he *should* have been having us do that. Apparently the guy was human after all.

But your mind plays tricks on you. Cautious as ever, I pulled some old history tests I'd saved out of the side pocket of my back-pack. To my relief, there were no initials—not on a single one. So it was true, and I didn't have it wrong. Apparently nobody initialed or identified themselves on the tests they corrected in history.

I smiled in Alysse's direction. If nobody knew who had corrected my test or anybody else's, I could still do the honest thing without getting Alysse in trouble. All I needed to do was tell Mr. Thorndike that *someone* had changed my answers and that I deserved an *F*, not an *A*. He wouldn't press me to tell him *who* had done it because he would assume I didn't know. How *would* I know? No, Mr. Thorndike would have no reason to believe I knew any more than he did who'd corrected my test. Even if he suspected Alysse, he would have absolutely no way of proving she'd corrected it.

But what if he came right out and asked me if I knew who had corrected my test? I chewed on my lower lip and then ground my back molars together once again. If he did for some reason ask me if I knew who had done it, I'd just tell him that I didn't want to get anyone in trouble. I almost laughed aloud with relief. It was all going to work out, after all. I could finally get the weights out of my feet and the freight train off my chest. In fact, maybe this was finally the answer I'd been waiting for. Just in case it was, I mouthed a quick thank you to Whoever might be listening in that other sphere.

Chapter Twenty

"Alysse, listen, I think I've just figured this out," I said immediately after Alvarez dismissed us. Even I could hear the relief in my voice. "Don't worry about anything, okay? It's all gonna work out. It's gonna be fine."

Alysse smiled patiently but not convincingly as she gathered up her notebook, pencils, and book. "Whatever you say, Armando."

"No, really, I'm not kidding." I followed her as she moved toward the door. When we entered the hall, the Beal twins called to her to come walk with them and Alysse did a peace sign in their direction, then turned and gave me the sign as well.

During lunch I was so relieved that everything was about to be resolved that I was almost giddy. I even joked around with Beezer, who generally irritated the socks off me. It wasn't like it would be fun telling Mr. Thorndike, of course, but at least there was now a way I could get out from under this thing. Fully intending to talk to him right after class, I went into history filled with determination.

Unfortunately, by the time I'd waited for some of my classmates to clear out, Kerrie, the girl with five hundred questions, was already up at Thorndike's desk. I lowered myself to Jen Fern's place and stayed there for a while, waiting patiently as the big hand on the clock continued to move. Mr. Hammond had started docking points each time we were tardy in orchestra because he was stressed about the holiday program. I opened and shut my hand a few times as the clock ticked on. Okay, time was up. I had to get to orchestra, and I had to get there fast. I would just have to return to Thorndike's room after school.

When I got back to Thorndike's less than an hour later, he was alone in the room, seated at his desk, and he seemed to be checking some things in his grade book. I readjusted my backpack and lowered my trombone case, my fingers slow to let go of the handle.

"Yes?" Up close, his wrinkles looked deeper, and his eyes under his thick brows appeared more old and tired than I'd expected. But when he saw it was me, his face seemed to lift a little. "Oh, hello, Mr. Archer." It had taken a while, but I was pretty sure the man was finally convinced that I was no troublemaker.

"Hello, Mr. Thorndike." I doubted he would feel quite so happy to see me after he'd heard what I had to say. "I, umm, need to talk with you about something." I lifted myself straighter, pulling in oxygen.

"Regarding?"

"Okay, ummm . . ." I plunged in. "I . . . umm . . . generally keep up pretty well in your class and do fairly well on the tests, but I wasn't prepared for this last test and, umm, well, I didn't do very well on it."

Mr. Thorndike entered a last notation into his book, then looked up at me again, his bushy eyebrows lowered in confusion. "Now, why would you say you didn't do well when you got the high in your class—a solid *A*? You were one of the few who did do well, by the way. I think your classmates will plan ahead a little better for the next test, don't you?"

I cleared my throat again and pushed my finger against my left eyelid, which was twitching. "Noooo, I didn't do well. I, uh . . ." This was the hard part. "I didn't get the high in the class, Mr. Thorndike, and I know for sure that I didn't get an *A* on that test or even anywhere near an *A*." I swallowed and then blurted it out. "I guessed on most of the answers and even left a bunch blank."

Mr. Thorndike pulled forward, his eyebrows together, his eyes narrowed. "Are you telling me that you cheated?"

"No. No, I don't cheat."

"Then I would be very interested in hearing your explanation."

This was the part that I needed to word carefully. "I guess someone filled in the answers for me as a joke or something."

Oops. I cringed at my choice of the word *joke.* I hadn't planned to use that word. *Joke* and *Alysse*—they were almost synonymous. Anyway, I was being deceitful. By using the word *someone,* I was making it sound like I didn't know who had corrected my test when I did know. I'd heard once that leading someone to believe something inaccurate was as dishonest as lying. My face was beginning to burn. I just wanted this to be over. Maybe this whole thing *was* deceitful when I knew full well who had corrected my test. Still, I hoped beyond hope that Thorndike wouldn't ask me now if I knew. Black and white? This was becoming more complicated by the second. Why had I thought this would work? "The point is," I continued quickly, my voice hoarse, "I mean, the reason I'm here is that, bottom line, I can't accept an *A* that I didn't earn."

Mr. Thorndike puffed forward his mouth and nodded. "So shall we assume that whoever corrected your test paper filled in your answers?"

I hesitated, but saw no reason I couldn't answer his question. "It looks that way."

"I see."

"So, anyway . . ." I took a step back, eager to finish this unpleasant task, get out of Mr. Thorndike's room, and get back to my life. "Basically, that's it. I just wanted to let you know so you could change my grade to an *F*."

"Well, I'm disappointed to hear that you performed poorly on the last test, Mr. Archer. I've come to expect more of you, but . . ." He folded his fingers together. "I appreciate your stepping forward with this information." I had the feeling he was actually quite amazed that I hadn't just accepted the higher grade. But Thorndike was Thorndike and not one to bend rules. "Let's go ahead, then, and change that grade right now. I'll make myself a note to get that entered into my computer. In the meantime, I've got my grade book right here. I like to keep two copies of grades, but, umm . . ." I wondered why he was hesitating and why he was still holding his pencil in the air. Thorndike chewed on his bottom lip for several seconds and then looked up. "Considering your past performance, I'm thinking I can give you the benefit of a doubt and that we can make that a *C* instead of an *F.*" He looked toward the door and lowered his voice. "I wouldn't do that for just anyone, you understand, but you've proven yourself to be a serious student. We can't, after all, know for a certainty that you failed this test."

"Thank you, but . . ." I *did* know for a certainty that I'd flunked. And yet Mr. Thorndike was looking at me with a don't-argue-with-a-rare-gift expression on his face. I started to nod, but then changed the direction of my head movement. "If you don't mind, I think I'd rather you went ahead and made that an *F.* My score at the max was twelve." After going to all this trouble, I needed to have the grade be accurate. I was a stickler myself, and I'd definitely missed more than half of the questions. "There's no question that I flunked it," I said unhappily.

Mr. Thorndike tipped his head, then lowered it into a single nod, his eyes cold again. "Very well, then." Quickly, and without further comment, Mr. Thorndike penciled in an *F,* then snapped his book shut. "As I said, I'll change it on my computer when I get home."

"Thank you, I, umm . . ." I decided to grovel. "I'll be better prepared next time."

"Yes, this mars your A-minus record in this class," he said. Now he sighed. "Well, at least you came forward, and that's more than most would have done."

Yeah, I'm kind of an idiot that way, I thought as I walked out of that class blowing air from my warm cheeks. Thank goodness it was over! I pulled my backpack up over one shoulder, readjusted my trombone case, and looked up and down the hall. Thorndike had reacted much better than I'd expected and hadn't seemed that angry. He'd probably been disappointed that I hadn't studied, and at first it had looked like it might get complicated, but it had turned out okay. *It's over*, I thought. I would go find Arnold, head home as fast as I could, get to my science project, finish my English, start immediately on the next history sections, and life would go on. I could maybe even think about Monica's wedding now. I'd pick up some Christmas gifts on the way to Lynette's and resume my life. I could think about stuff like that now. I could really dig in at the warehouse over the weekend and practice for the Christmas performance first thing in the morning. As I hurried toward my locker, there was a little bounce in my step again. Yes! It was over!

Only it wasn't over.

Chapter Twenty-One

I could tell by the way Mr. Thorndike walked into the class-room on Monday afternoon that he was wearing war paint. He always peered at us over his glasses, but this time his head seemed to be jerking up and down, making him look like he literally had four eyes. I hoped beyond hope that this foul mood didn't have anything to do with what I'd admitted to him Friday after school, that this was about something else entirely. I assured myself that there were any number of things that could have aggravated Mr. Thorndike. Maybe there'd been some behavior problem in his previous class. Maybe his oatmeal had burned that morning. Maybe one of the younger teachers had made a crack about his bow tie. Oh, how I hoped something else had soured his disposition even more than it was generally soured.

Mr. Thorndike called the roll crisply, then snapped shut the thick brown roll book and looked around the classroom. "Before we begin our history lesson today, I have some business to take care of," he said.

I pressed my fingers against the front edge of the desktop, my eyes on his face.

"Last week," he said, enunciating carefully, "you corrected one another's tests. As you are aware, I have felt you were mature enough to handle this small assignment, and so far we've had no problems."

Slowly, I moved my body in reverse until I reached the back of my seat.

In a low and controlled voice, Mr. Thorndike continued. "Unfortunately, this is apparently not the case. Friday after school, Mr. Kendall Archer reported to me that whoever corrected his test filled in the questions he'd left blank, giving Kendall a grade he didn't deserve." As Mr. Thorndike removed his glasses, I felt the urge to slide down my chair and into the floor, maybe hoping to disappear into some invisible drain.

"Now I need to know who that person was," said Mr. Thorndike, peering around the room.

Even if there'd been a drain nearby, my head didn't feel like it would have gotten through. It felt strangely heavy . . . huge . . . my face the heaviest of all. My eyelids had turned to rock and had fallen shut. It was just as well, because it was important for me not to look in Allyson's direction. Even though I wanted in the worst way to know how she was reacting, glancing at her now could give her away. I hoped as well that the people around her weren't look-ing at her either. I managed to lift my eyelids far enough to check with my peripheral vision and could tell she wasn't moving. Nobody was.

"Let me continue," Mr. Thorndike said, his lips pulled tight against those sharp incisors. "If that person does not identify himself or herself, the entire class will be punished. I am not just talking about an extra assignment, students. This will be far more consequential than anything I've meted out before. We're talking about permanent records. If someone does not step forward and admit to this, the grade of every person in this class will be lowered and poor citizenship marks issued. And that will be only the beginning. It could very well be that graduations in several cases will be jeopardized. Now, I will ask you one more time. Who," and he looked around slowly, "corrected Mr. Archer's test last Wednesday?"

My fingers were pressing so hard against the desk that pain would have been shooting up my arms if they'd had any feeling. Was I moaning out loud or just inside? *Nooooo!* I was saying with my entire body. *This can't be happening!* It was the absolute last thing I wanted to have happen. The absolute last thing. The tension in the room could almost have been sliced with a spoon as students darted looks at each other. Molly and Jake and the others around Alysse, however, continued staring straight ahead. No one spoke. In fact, the only sound that broke the silence was the hum of the clock.

I moved ever so slightly to alleviate the pressure in my chest, and lifted my neck to help me swallow. From the corner of my eye, I could see Alysse move slightly as well. She sat up a little. Then she opened her mouth.

"Look . . . I . . ." At first I didn't even realize I was speaking. It felt almost as if someone else was talking out of my mouth. But then I knew it had to be me because I recognized my voice, and my tongue and lips were moving. "Sir, I didn't want anyone to get into trouble."

Mr. Thorndike twisted his head in my direction so fast he looked like something out of a Halloween poltergeist movie. "Oh, but you didn't get anyone in trouble, Mr. Archer." He took in the rest of the class again. "Let me make it clear, class, that whoever did this got *himself* into trouble—himself or herself." Was it just my imagination, or had he just glanced in Alysse's direction? "Now, I'm asking you just one last time," he said slowly, pausing between each word. "Who filled in the answers on Mr. Archer's test last Wednesday?"

"I said I didn't want to get anyone in trouble," I heard myself repeat firmly, my voice louder this time, its forcefulness surprising even me.

It was clear by the way he blinked hard and then jerked in my direction that Mr. Thorndike felt I'd just jumped way over that invisible line of what he deemed acceptable. Thorndike pushed his glasses back and leaned much farther forward than he generally did when he was about to pounce on someone for an infraction. I was in for it—oh, yes, I was really in for it. But oddly, I didn't care. I was ready for him to dish out his wrath at me and wasn't trembling in my boots as I would have been doing under normal circumstances. Maybe I even hoped that drawing his anger in my direction would shift the attention away from Allyson. I drew in my breath and this time shut my eyes as I waited for him to come

145

down hard. But before Mr. Thorndike had a chance to lash out at me, a familiar voice rang out clearly. "I corrected Kendall's test, Mr. Thorndike. It was me. I did it."

Our teacher turned his head toward Alysse so slowly we could have finished a plate of spaghetti by the time his eyes reached her. With great relish, he finally spoke. "Well, well, Allyson Pringle . . ." His voice remained calm, but it was obvious by the way his right eye was flinching that this calm was deceptive. "So you're saying that you corrected Mr. Archer's test a few days ago?"

"Yes, I did."

The corners of Thorndike's mouth began twitching now. "Well, well," he repeated, still slowly and with great satisfaction. "I should have known. Yes, I really should have known."

"It was meant as a joke," Alysse added, her face expressionless. Molly stared at Mr. Thorndike wide-eyed as Jen concentrated on something on her desk. Jake opened and closed his right hand. I really needed to swallow again, but couldn't seem to manage this simple bodily function because my tongue felt like it had swollen to the size of a baseball.

Mr. Thorndike's nostrils were flared, and his left eye was twitching now. He seemed to be nodding again. "I see," he said even more slowly, "so it was just a joke. Just a joke." He looked around the room. "Is this surprising, class?" Since he didn't get so much as a head bob, he answered his own question. "I don't find it at all surprising, Miss Pringle, because you've clearly established that you're very good at joking, haven't you?"

As Mr. Thorndike leaned forward, his palms on his desk, his voice gradually increased in volume and intensity. "Haven't you,

Miss Pringle?" He paused. "From the first, or was it the second, day of this school year, you've made that clear. As I recall, I even had to send you home at one point. Oh, you've tried to make a good impression on the students and you've even won over certain members of the faculty. You've been able to get away with your shenanigans because every once in a while you've done something . . ." He made quote signs with his fingers: "benevolent."

It angered me that he was probably referring to homecoming and Charlotte. Why couldn't he see things as they really were? Alysse *was* benevolent.

"Well, this time, young lady," he continued, "there's no smoke screen. Your joking has just gotten you into serious trouble." He was quiet again, but lethally so. Thorndike picked a pencil up from his desk and tapped it, then pointed it at Alysse, his mouth lifted into a snarl. "I've had just about enough trouble out of you, and I'm tired, very tired of this kind of behavior. It isn't humorous, and it isn't appropriate." He took in the rest of us, his jaw stiff. "You're juniors and seniors now, and it's time for you to get serious about life. I have absolutely no tolerance for this kind of mischief and won't allow it in my classroom." Mr. Thorndike slammed his palms down with a thump. "Miss Pringle, this antic is not only going to affect your grade and your citizenship, but it may have just cost you your leadership position and your graduation status. You and I will be having a talk with Mrs. Millenstein as soon as possible. Please report to my desk immediately after class."

"Whatever you say," said Alysse stonily.

I was so horrified at this unexpected turn of events that for the remainder of the period I stared down at the sheet of paper in my notebook, at my textbook, anywhere but at Alysse or my class-mates. It was a well-known fact that Mrs. Millenstein almost always supported the teachers when it came to problems involv-ing students. I'd never heard of a case where she hadn't. My stom-ach had risen to my chest, squeezing at my lungs as I tried to breathe. Trouble like this could affect Allyson's dream of being accepted to a top drama school. And would she really be ousted from her school office? Could Thorndike do that?

There are moments in a person's life that stand still. I felt as if I were stuck in the center of an out-of-control horror merry-go-round. Yet, on the surface, as class continued, I went through the motions, taking notes, acting as if I was listening. Later, when I looked back at the words I'd written in my notebook that day in history, they made little or no sense.

It wasn't until class was almost over that I managed to regain a little equilibrium. When the bell rang I hurried to the front of the classroom. "Mr. Thorndike," I said, talking fast. "I'd like to ask you to reconsider and let this go. Alysse, umm, Allyson is doing a really good job in her position as a class officer. I know it's hard some-times for teachers to . . ." I wasn't at all sure where I was heading with this speech. "Sir, I'd really appreciate it if you'd give her a break—another chance."

"A break? Oh, but I've given Miss Pringle many 'breaks,' as you call them."

"Yes, but—"

"I've given Allyson Pringle more chances than she or any stu-dent deserves. That will be enough, Mr. Archer." He didn't even bother looking up.

"But . . ."

"You're excused, Mr. Archer."

"But . . ."

His eyes had turned to ice. "I said, that will be enough!" Then he looked toward Alysse, who was waiting patiently several yards from us. "Miss Pringle, my desk, please."

My head throbbing, my mouth open, I was half afraid I might be sick right there at his desk. I had no choice but to leave. I took a few steps back, stopped, glanced toward Alysse, opened my mouth, and then turned to go. A few other students filtered out quietly as well, some looking straight forward, others glancing back. "Nice one, Archer," Danny Karlowski muttered when I passed him in the doorway.

"Yeah, good job!" Bret Nuswander bumped into me hard. I didn't go flying like I had a few years before, but I didn't push him back, either. I just rolled away and moved on.

"Good job all right, Archer," I muttered to myself after I turned at the AB hall, my legs moving and the rest of me following along. "Really good job."

In orchestra I went through the motions and that was about it. When it was time to put my trombone away, I felt so drained of strength that I couldn't bring myself to reach for my case. It felt as if there were an anchor tied to my feet and that my arms and hands, even my tongue and jaw, were attached somehow to that anchor, making it impossible for me to move. Why, I wondered, hadn't I listened to Arnold? Why hadn't I just left all this alone? It was all my fault this had happened. By trying to do what I'd thought was the right thing, I had created a nightmare. I was far too conscientious—always such a stickler. My brother was right. Arnold was right. Alysse was right. She'd just been trying to be funny and I'd had to make a big issue of it. I could have worked it out. I could have just accepted the *A* and then purposely missed a bunch on the next history test. Yes, that was what I should have done. So why was I just realizing that now? If only I had just kept my mouth shut, everything would have ended up fine. But no, I hadn't been smart enough to do that.

Instead of heading to my locker after school, I turned at the front hall in the direction of the office. If I could talk to Mrs. Millenstein before Thorndike got to her, maybe it would help. "Could I help you, dear?" asked the middle-aged secretary at the front desk. Because she so obviously cared about us, students pretty much overlooked the strange way she drew on her eyebrows and puffed up her hair.

"Is Mrs. Millenstein here?"

"Oh, I'm sorry, but Mrs. Millenstein had to leave early for an appointment. Do you think you could come back in the morning?"

"Okay." I felt a little more optimistic and hopeful. If Mrs. Millenstein had left, it meant Mr. Thorndike wouldn't have been able to set up a meeting with her. Or had he already talked with her?

As soon as I got home from school, Lucky Duck rushed past me out the back door, reminding me that Mom was still in New York with Dad. "Sorry, mutt," I muttered miserably.

I threw my stuff on the kitchen table, pulled off my hat and gloves and coat, hung up the key on the key rack, then moved into the family room area, where I picked up the remote, flipped on the TV, and plopped down in front of it.

Two, maybe three minutes later, Lucky was scratching on the door to let me know that he wanted back in. I didn't blame him. It was cold out there. I pulled one foot and then the other to the floor, forced myself upright, and finally trudged to the kitchen, opening the back door just far enough for him to slip through.

Lucky followed me back into the family room to the couch, where I plopped down again. Watching television wasn't part of my normal after-school routine, and he whined a little. I ignored him as I sat staring at the flickering screen. I'm not sure how long I would have sat there if the phone hadn't rung. I forced myself up again. By the time I found it in the plant stand, it had stopped ringing. But the caller ID said it was Dad's warehouse. Bob, probably. I'd need to call him back. Instead I just stood there, the phone in one hand and the remote in the other. Lucky Duck nudged me. "Yeah, okay. There might be a problem." I clicked the TV off.

Sure enough, Bob had some questions about an order of circuit-breaker panels going to Kansas. I knew which order he was talking about and explained the situation. After I clicked him off, I stared at the phone in my hand. I wanted in the worst way to call Alysse. Even though we'd done most of our talking in school, and on an occasional e-mail, I'd memorized her number. Now I slowly tapped all the digits but the last, which I couldn't bring myself to push. I was too afraid of how she would respond. I was afraid Alysse wouldn't want to talk to me—not now. Not ever.

My cell was about out of juice, so I took the wireless downstairs with me and lay down on my bed for a few seconds. Then I jumped back up and went into the computer/sewing room. I'd seen a stake directory by the computer—sure enough, I found it in the desk basket under some spools of thread and an old ward bulletin. I pulled it out and flipped to the Cs. Did I dare call Sister Carruber? She'd been pretty excited when I'd gotten nominated for the Spirit of Hollenda award. Maybe I could tell her that Alysse was the one who had helped me get nominated. Maybe I could tell her about what had happened in Thorndike's and explain that it had just been a prank—a crazy practical joke—that Alysse was a little impulsive but a great leader and a good person. Maybe Mrs. Carru could then talk to Mrs. Millenstein. I tapped the numbers and pushed the green "talk" button. The phone rang several times, and I was about to hang up when a young voice answered. "Oh, hi, is Mrs. Carruber there?" I asked quickly. "I mean, is Sister Carruber there?"

"Gwamma's at store. She buy me yummy fwuit smacks."

"Okay." I smiled in spite of my misery. "Okay, thanks." I looked at the oversized clock on the wall next to the door and wondered how soon I could call again. It was family night, so I didn't dare wait too long. The computer was right there in front of me and I dropped down into the seat. Like it or not, I needed to enter the business invoices. I placed the phone next to the keyboard and went to work.

When the phone rang about twenty minutes later, I grabbed it fast.

"Hi, Kenny," said my mother, almost breathless. "I don't have long to talk, but I just wanted to make sure you're doing okay. Did you get the bridesmaids' dresses to your sister? Oh, and have you been getting in the mail?"

Even though I'd hoped it was Mrs. Carru, it felt good to hear from my mother. I missed her and Dad. "Yeah, no worry on both counts. I got the stuff to Lynette's a couple of days ago. That lady she knows was going to start work on the dresses Saturday."

"Oh, good, good."

"As far as the mail, we've mostly gotten ads and a few bills. I'll take care of the business ones."

"Okay," Mom sighed with relief. "I'm glad you remembered to get those dresses to Lynette's. But then, I knew you would. How are things going otherwise? How's my boy?"

"How are things going over *there?*" I asked, sidestepping.

"Oh, Kenny, this is such an incredible place!" my mother raved. "We visited Rockefeller Plaza this weekend and went to church near the temple. While Dad made some calls, I explored a little. There was an area of nice little shops not far from the hotel and I found some things we hadn't picked up yet for the wedding, and guess what else I found?" She began describing some buttons that JoAnn's fabric store in Kalamazoo had run out of. Next she told me about some tips the shopkeeper, who'd once been a seamstress, gave her that she knew would help with the lace trim she'd been struggling with on the wedding dress. "I really think this was meant to be because this woman once lived in Ann Arbor and

when I told her I was from nearby she was very friendly and help-
ful. So some people might look at that as a coincidence, but I know
better. I'm so glad I came with Dad. I almost didn't come with him
because we're so close to the wedding and I told him it was ridicu-
lous for me to go, but I'm so glad I did. Dad was completely right
that I needed to take a break for a day or two and now that this has
happened, well, I always said your father is inspired when it comes
to these kinds of things. The only thing is, I keep wishing all you
kids were here. We're going to try to get into a Broadway play
tonight with the Talbots who live in Palmyra and are driving over
here. They know the locals' secrets on getting into plays. For sure
we'll come again when you can come. In fact, I want all you kids
to come when the business is doing better. Would you like that?"

"Now, what?" I realized I'd tuned out.

"Are you okay, Kenny?"

The phone beeped before I could answer. Not that I had any
intention of telling her my problems right now when she was so
up about life and this little trip. But mothers tend to read your
mind, even at long distances. Besides, I needed to talk to Mrs.
Carruber. "Uh-oh, there's the other line," I said anxiously. "I'm
glad you're having a great time."

"All right, honey, but are you sure you're okay? You've got
enough to eat, haven't you?"

"Yeah, yeah, there's plenty."

"Okay, then. You take care of yourself. Love you. 'Bye now."

"Okay, Mom, love you too."

I quickly pushed the flash button then, but it was too late.

When the phone rang again two seconds later, I could see that it was Arnold. I stared at it as it rang, but didn't press the answer but-ton. I really didn't want to talk to my friend right then. Maybe he wouldn't come right out and say the words *I told you*, but I'd know he was thinking them. Lynette called next, and again I didn't answer. She'd said something on Friday about joining them for family night, but I didn't think I was up to it. I wasn't up to much of anything.

I went back upstairs and turned on the television again, imme-diately recognizing a character from one of the *CSI* shows. Since I really wasn't in the mood to look at any dead bodies, I clicked the channel again and then again. Lucky Duck, who still seemed con-fused that I wasn't following normal procedure, let out a tiny whine of concern. Or was he hungry? I forced myself off the couch and checked his bowl in the kitchen, which looked like it still had plenty of food in it. "Go downstairs if you're tired," I said, collaps-ing back on the couch. Lucky just stood there staring at me, still whining softly. "Okay, fine!"

Forcing myself off the couch again, I dragged down the steps, then threw myself on my bed without even bothering to take off my boots. A few seconds later I heard Lucky's feet on the stairs, and the sound was almost comforting. "I'm not doing so great, Duck," I said when he flopped down on the rug next to the bed.

Once again something reminded me that it wasn't my dog I needed to be talking to. But I couldn't bring myself to move off the bed and get down on my knees. Maybe I just didn't have the faith that even He could help me at this point. Maybe I'd come to believe that some problems were hopeless and that this was one of them. But then I remembered something, and I glanced over at the quote on my bulletin board, which I'd copied from the board in seminary earlier in the year: "The times you feel like praying least are the times you need to be praying most." It was right next to the petal Alysse had given me at Halloween and my dried boutonniere from the winter dance. I snorted softly. The dance. It was hard to believe it had been less than two weeks before that Alysse and I had had such a good time at the Winter Wonderland dance. It seemed more like eons ago in some other life.

I pushed myself off the bed to the throw rug on the floor next to it and knelt there for a long time, unable to form words. Finally I remembered that God hears all prayers, verbal or not, and I began to plead soundlessly, wordlessly for help. I felt a little better after I got back up—better enough anyway to get out my Spanish and English books so I could stare at the covers.

The next morning I woke up so late that I realized I was not only not going to make it to any of seminary, but I wouldn't even make it to school early enough to talk to Mrs. Carru or Mrs. Millenstein like I'd planned. It was generally my turn to drive on Tuesdays, but Arnold had told me we'd need to be on our own because he had an appointment with his math teacher about his grade. I barely had ten minutes to get dressed and out the door. Man, had I messed up! I rushed to the bathroom, patted down my hair, grabbed my toothbrush and some toothpaste, then threw on my clothes.

"Keeping late hours studying, huh?" said Mrs. Cavanaugh about fifteen minutes later. "Well, you're in luck, sailor. I haven't sent the cards to the office yet."

I made it to my seat but I couldn't bring myself to look around and was glad when Mrs. Cavanaugh handed me the customary work sheet so I could concentrate on that.

Chapter Twenty-Two

Alysse was already at her desk by the time I got to Spanish. I couldn't see her face because her hair was draped over it, and she was once again digging through her Minnie Mouse bag. "Alysse?" I touched her shoulder. "I'm really sorry about what happened in history yesterday. I thought I'd figured it all out. I had no idea Thorndike would react that way." I paused for several seconds. "I'm . . . I'm . . ." I was feeling like I might throw up.

Alysse lifted her head, pushed back her hair, and attempted to smile. But even though she was wearing her standard red glasses, I could tell the smile hadn't made it to her eyes. "Hey, don't worry about it, Archer. It's no big deal." She was trying to sound light and unaffected, but she was clearly faking it.

"So what happened after class?"

"Not much. Mr. Thorndike and I have an appointment with Mrs. Millenstein later this afternoon, so I guess I'll be finding out more then. I don't know how Thorndike's feeling today, but he wasn't Mr. Happy yesterday, was he?"

"You know I didn't want anything like that to happen. You know I would have taken a fist in the gut before I would have had this happen."

She widened her eyes. "Whoa! Hey, we've got to get you back up there on a stage! Such drama!"

"No, I—"

"Listen, I said don't worry about it, okay? It doesn't matter."

But it did matter. It mattered to me, and I could tell it mattered to Alysse. In fact, her mentioning the stage sent additional concern stampeding through me. The play! I hadn't thought about that. Heat rushed to my head. Could she get tossed from *Bye Bye Birdie* as well? What if there was a citizenship requirement of some kind? I didn't want to go there. I couldn't go there. It was terrible enough that she could possibly be ousted from her office. That alone was unthinkable.

"What do you think they'll do to you?"

"I'm hoping that at the most Millenstein puts me on probation, but if I'm booted from my office, then I'm booted."

"Don't say that."

"Hey, Thorndike's right. I've been asking for it."

Daphne, who'd apparently been listening in on our conversation, flipped around at this point. "Well, maybe Alysse is going to be nice about this," she spat out, "but you don't want to know what the rest of us think of you."

"Chill out, Daphne. I told you he didn't know this would happen," Alysse snapped back.

"Fine, I'll chill out for now," Daphne said. "But if they don't let you stay in as an officer, I'm sorry, but I'm not going to be chilling out." Daphne continued glowering at me.

For the rest of the class period, I had trouble concentrating. Not only Daphne, but Dee Dee, Rhonda, and several others threw me looks of disgust. I could feel Lakeesha's eyes lasering into my back. Carlin glanced back once and he wasn't smiling. After class Tallulah barely acknowledged me and Dansco, who just the day before had tapped my knuckles, now just nodded smilelessly in my direction. Word was apparently out there already—just like that, that fast. Maybe the yell leaders *would* end up doing that "Kick Kendall Archer" cheer Arnold had demonstrated.

In the cafeteria Patrice snapped her head toward the far wall the second she saw me. It looked like I wasn't her "Kenny" anymore.

It was an odd thing, though. I wasn't nearly as worried about how my classmates were reacting to me as I was about what was going to happen to Alysse, who even now was sticking up for me. I was desperate to think of a way to repair what I'd done. There had to be some way I could fix things.

After lunch, Nate Manicox pushed into my shoulder just as I was about to turn into AB hall. I'd forgotten how huge this guy was. "Hey, I heard you snitched on Alysse, and you know what? This is what." His breath in my face, he knocked into me again and my shoulder rammed against a locker.

This was feeling all too familiar, bringing back memories I didn't want brought back. Big or not, I pushed Nate back in what

I'm sorry to say wasn't your most Christian manner. "Fight!" I heard somebody yell behind me.

I straightened my shoulders, stepped back, and lifted my hand. There wasn't going to be any fight. "Look, I'm just trying to get to my next class. I don't want any trouble."

"Oh yeah, maggot? Well, you should have thought of that before you fouled up Alysse."

Nate lunged into me once more—hard. I landed against the lockers again and this time banged my elbow. Okay, this wasn't working. I felt myself jerk forward, my hands forming fists. I'm not sure what I would have done next, but I didn't have a chance to find out because Alysse had come out of nowhere and was standing between Nate and me, or, I should say, *prancing* between us.

"Hey, Manicox, you want a piece of somebody, you can deal with me!" Alysse taunted, punching into the air, her shoulders down. "I'm Laila Ali, baby; I'm Rockette Balboa." Circling Nate, Alysse sucker-punched him softly in the stomach, then fake punched him with a right, then a left. A group that was gathering began whooping and laughing as, head down, she went after Nate with a barrage of air punches. When Nate lifted his head, I could see that he was trying hard not to laugh but wasn't having much success. Snickering, he lifted his hand and backed away. Her job almost complete, Alysse shook her arms like a pro boxer and then fake punched him one additional time. "We'll hang out tonight, okay, big guy, but only if you keep the testosterone in check. And you can tell Ren and the rest of your overgrown buddies the same thing."

Nate wasn't laughing so much that he couldn't give me a

threatening look as he backed down the hall. He pointed at me as he turned the corner. "We're not finished."

"You're *re*finished!" she called after him.

"So, you okay?" she asked me after Nate had turned the corner.

I shook my head and stretched my arms as I tried to control my trembling. "I think I can take care of myself, thanks. You don't need to put on any Rockella or whatever performances for me."

"Yeah, you guys are *all* overdosed on testosterone," Alysse snorted. Straightening her red glasses, she grinned at the group still gathered. "Hey, I coulda been a contender, huh?" Turning toward me again, she said quietly, "Just watch your back."

"I'm not worried," I said, my voice still not cooperating. I shook my head. "I mean, I'm not worried about your jock friends. I *am* worried about coming up with something to get you out of this mess I got you in. I've still got to find a way to fix all this, but don't worry, I'll think of something."

"That's what they told Humpty Dumpty," she replied.

"Yeah, well, there's gotta be something."

Mrs. Carru was actually my only real shot, I decided less than fifteen minutes later. Millenstein was so hard-nosed that getting through to her would be like trying to chisel through concrete. Alysse hadn't said the exact time of her appointment, and I was wishing I'd asked. She also hadn't mentioned if parents were involved.

During my lunch hour I hurried to the office, but this time, the cheerful secretary let me know that Mrs. Carruber had had to go to a district meeting. I rushed back after school before a tutoring session only to find out that the meeting had apparently lasted too long for my former Primary leader to get back to her office. Sensing my anxiety, the secretary patted my hand. "We'll get you taken care of, honey, don't you worry."

"Yeah, well, tomorrow might be too late," I muttered, heading out. I turned around, remembering my manners. "But thanks."

After clearing up some problems at Dad's warehouse, I headed home, where again I let the dog out back. It had snowed while I was in school, and I went out with Lucky to find the shovel so I could hit the sidewalks. Five minutes later I was pushing it through the heavy snow. It felt almost good to have something to keep my body busy and exerted. But soon my hands and feet began to throb and I was glad to get the job done and head inside. Lucky seemed to feel the same and began licking the ice off his feet.

Since I hadn't done anything about my homework the day before, not even my Spanish, I had no choice but to force myself to head downstairs. There was a lot left to do before we left for Monica's reception, and I knew it wasn't going to be easy to concentrate. I'd barely begun my English when I realized I wasn't going to be able to do any homework until I figured something out. I was so not with it that I was half afraid I'd leave my parents stranded at the airport. They were scheduled to arrive at 7:30, and I was to meet them at 7:50.

Should I call Monica to see if she could think of anything I could do to repair the mess I'd made for Alysse? I lifted my eyes. What made me think she'd have time to deal with my problems when she was getting married at the end of the week? Lynette was out as well; she would be getting the baby ready for bed. Kip already thought I was a big dweeb and would tell me I worried too much. I couldn't call Arnold, either. After all, he'd tried to warn me. No, this was *my* problem.

I tried again to study, started flipping through an old *Time* magazine, and tossed it across the room. The phone was still in my room from the night before, and Mrs. Carru's number was right there on my mother's stick-on notepad. I wasn't sure what good it would do to talk to Mrs. Carru if Thorndike and Alysse had already met with Mrs. Millenstein that afternoon, but I found myself dialing. Once again I got Carru's machine, but I hung up before it had completed the message. But then I found myself wishing I'd left her a message, so I pressed "redial." This time when I got the machine I heard myself pouring out the entire story, my voice high and whiny. After I finally hung up, I couldn't believe what I'd done, and I clenched my teeth and shut my eyes. Why was I pouring out my guts on a message machine? The woman had kids and grandkids! But I didn't have much time to worry about it because when I glanced at the clock, I realized that I needed to get the heck out of there and hightail it to the airport to pick up my parents.

Chapter Twenty-Three

"How are things going for you, Kip . . . umm, Kendall?" Brother Aspen asked me after seminary the next morning. At least he was correcting himself faster now. "We missed you yesterday and you seem tired again."

It was actually a miracle I was in seminary. My parents' flight had been delayed over three hours, thanks to a major storm in the New York area, and we hadn't pulled into the driveway until midnight. They felt bad I'd had to sit there at the airport waiting that long and had been as happy as I was to finally get home and into bed.

"Fine. Things are fine," I told Brother Aspen. I realized I was lying to my seminary teacher and I repented immediately. "Okay, not fine."

"Have you decided if you want to talk about your problem?"

"Maybe later. Right now I need to get to school."

"Well, I'm available, son."

I nodded. "Thanks."

He patted my shoulder. "And you know Who is always available to us anytime, anywhere."

I nodded again. "Yeah, yeah, I do." And I did know who he meant, and it wasn't Sister/Mrs. Carru. Nevertheless, I still wanted to talk to my former Primary president, just in case.

Arnold had band practice before school again, but even though our other car was in the shop, Mom had said she'd be home all day unpacking, washing, and working on the bridal gown and I was welcome to take the van.

I found a space in the parking lot fairly close to the side door of the school. Avoiding the front hall, I hurried to the office the long way. There were several students waiting and I glanced nervously at the clock.

"Mrs. Carruber's booked," one of the student assistants, a girl with white streaks in her black hair, said brusquely when it was my turn. Had she already heard about what had happened with Alysse? Or was I just becoming paranoid?

"Okay, thanks." I turned, walked out of the office foyer door, and headed to English, late again. To my relief they were still doing announcements.

Mrs. Cavanaugh pulled her eyes from the screen, glanced at me, then quickly looked back up. Fantasia pulled back in her seat when she saw me, and April whispered something to the guy next to her. Several others shifted in their seats. I lifted my eyes and immediately knew why everyone was acting so weird. Above us, Sam Penosh was being announced as the winner the Spirit of Hollenda award. I headed to my seat, forcing myself to act normal.

I'd had no delusions whatsoever that I would win, but Sam Penosh? The guy was a drug dealer.

As I lowered myself into my seat, I felt other eyes on me as well, but there were no condolences. What a contrast to when I had been nominated! But that was then. It shouldn't have amazed me that people in English already seemed to know what had happened in history the day before yesterday. The guy next to me was cracking his knuckles; when I looked over, he started messing with his folder. He too seemed to already know. The whole class seemed to know. Again, it didn't matter. I just wanted things to be all right with Alysse.

"So what happened?" I asked her anxiously as soon as I got to third period. "Did you meet with anybody yesterday?"

"No, the meeting was postponed and we met this morning first thing," Alysse said, her voice tired. "It wasn't too bad. I was given citizenship demerits and I was docked big-time points from history, and, umm . . ." she hesitated. "I got temporarily relieved of my SBO duties."

My heart did a nosedive. "How temporarily?"

"The good news is that Lindsey volunteered to take over for me and that's been okayed. She'll handle my assignments along with her historian responsibilities, and the other officers all offered to pitch in as well. If I behave and there are no more 'infractions,' I can maybe be reinstated before the end of the school year. First I need to do about a thousand hours of school and community service, though."

I drooped down in my seat, my insides still smashed together, my head light. "This isn't what I was hoping to hear."

"Hey, listen, it could have been much worse," Alysse continued. "Thorndike was pushing for me to be relieved of my office for good, so he wasn't too happy with the decision. Believe me, if he'd had his way, I'd maybe even be expelled. Hey, who am I kidding? If he had his way, I'd be heading to the state prison."

I didn't laugh. "You think they'll for sure reinstate you, then?"

"As soon as I meet the requirements. I just feel lucky that Mrs. Millenstein had a conflict and Mrs. Carruber stood in for her. I think Millenstein would have booted me out of my office permanently. Carru's a lot more lenient. She seemed to understand that it was a practical joke—a stupid practical joke, but a joke."

I rounded my lips and exhaled slowly. I had the feeling it was *Sister* and not *Mrs.* Carru who'd showed up to work that day. Maybe the lame message I'd left had done some good after all.

Alysse pulled in a breath and made an effort to smile, but there was still that weariness in her voice when she said, "I told you that you didn't need to worry about it."

"I'll stop worrying when they reinstate you."

Rhonda, a few seats over, and Daphne didn't look like they thought it could have been much worse. Neither did the others in our class. In fact, if kids in our school were upset before, they were furious when word got around that Alysse had been relieved of her office temporarily. As I walked down the halls of school, I could kind of tell that the "Kendall Archer is a cool, funny guy" period had come to an end. I was getting looks now that would have made a pit bull yelp.

"Better steer clear of me for a while," I told Arnold.

"I can handle it," Arnold said.

And I honestly thought *I* could handle it all as well: the looks, the verbal thrashing, maybe even a bump or two here and there, as long as Alysse continued to be my friend. As long as she was still okay with me, I was pretty sure I could take anything dished out to me. But in Spanish that next day even Alysse seemed to be acting differently toward me. As Rhonda talked to her about a party that weekend, Alysse didn't even glance in my direction. And the following day—the day I needed to check out early because of the wedding—Alysse seemed remote. Oh, she was civil and said hello and so forth. She didn't ignore me or anything. It was nothing I could pinpoint, just something I could sense.

Chapter Twenty-Four

That Friday afternoon Mom, Dad, Lynette, Josh, Baby Skipper, and I caught a flight to Salt Lake. We rented a Dodge Caravan at a rental place near the Salt Lake airport and took I-15 to our motel in Provo. Early the next day we drove the additional fifteen minutes or so to Payson, Rulon's hometown, where we helped set up for the reception. On the way, Dad complained to Mom about how much everything was costing. Mom worried aloud about the dresses fitting okay, especially Monica's wedding gown. My thoughts were back home in Kalamazoo.

Seeing good old Monica again did, I have to say, soothe my soul. It took me a few seconds longer than the rest of the family to get into the house, thanks to all the stuff I was hauling in, but when I got inside Monica called out, "Kendall!" and grabbed me for a breath-defying bear hug. Then she spun me in the direction of Rulon, who was moving toward me, his hand outstretched. "Kenny, this is my wonderful fiancé, Rulon, the love of my life," she gushed. I lowered the bags and held out my hand. "And Rulon, this is my fantastic brother Kendall!" Her words made my eyes well up. But none of this was supposed to be about me, and I pulled myself together fast. I knew how anxious Monica was to have us all get to know her "prince," and I have to say that Rulon seemed like a nice enough guy. He was more than just a couple of inches shorter than Monica, however, like she'd claimed. He was more like four or five inches shorter. But hey, there weren't a whole lot of people taller than my sister. With the exception of Kip, Monica was the tallest in our family. I'd long ago given up hoping to catch up with Kip, and my goal had become trying to catch up with Monica, which I hoped to do during my mission. Rulon, however, was back from a mission, and so I doubted he'd be growing more. But so what? If Monica didn't care, why should anybody else?

"So, you play any sports?" I asked him. It was the kind of thing my brother would have asked had he been there, but Kip had just started a new job and he and his family wouldn't be joining us until the reception in Kalamazoo.

"Just Church ball," Rulon said, pushing back his glasses, "but I'm not very good." It was probably a good thing Kip wasn't there to hear that, but I liked the guy for leveling. And hey, I related.

I liked it even better when Rulon beamed up at my sister and said, "I'm just glad somebody in this new family will be holding up the sports end of things. Monica has amazing talent, and I plan to support her in whatever she decides to do. You're looking at her number-one fan." The guy was now a stud as far as I was concerned.

The ceremony was beautiful, according to my parents, and the reception in Payson, the journey home, and then the second reception in Kalamazoo all went off without a hitch. There wasn't a hitch I was aware of, anyway. Later, Mom told me that more people had shown up than they'd expected at the Kalamazoo reception, and they'd had to begin cutting the lower layer of the cake before the evening was even half over. Then there'd been something with the flowers. But even Mom, I could tell, felt good about how things had turned out. The main thing was that none of the challenges fazed my sister, who continued looking as elated as she'd sounded on the phone when she'd first told us she was getting married.

Gathering the gifts, setting up and taking down, keeping track of the little kids, and concentrating on the happy couple helped me to forget temporarily about what had happened with Alysse. But under the surface it was still there, like background noise. I tried to continue thinking about happy things, I really did. But as soon as the two lovebirds had made their escape and we'd cleaned up and loaded things into our van and it was all over, I was right back in a funk.

Since we hadn't fully celebrated Christmas, my family and I opened a few gifts on New Year's Day. And then that Monday, in the middle of one of Michigan's worst snowstorms, I returned to Hollenda to finish up the last two weeks of the semester.

I'll sum it up like this: Those two weeks were not the best of my life. The one good aspect about being an outcast? I had plenty of time to catch up, study for finals, get term papers in, and do the finishing touches on my science project—a balsa-wood bridge that, despite the fact that the rest of my life seemed to be falling apart, turned out to be a strong one.

During the school hours themselves, I concentrated on just making it through. Poor Señor Alvarez undoubtedly wondered what had happened to our happy-go-lucky group and why we weren't having as much fun anymore. As far as history—*tense* isn't a strong enough word.

I generally tutored during lunch on Tuesdays, but Artie, who'd showed up only once in a while anyway, didn't make it back to school after the break. Juan Phineas stopped me in the hall to let me know he'd be switching lunches and would go ahead and have somebody else tutor him. Juan had been making good progress, and I was relieved when I saw him with one of the other tutors later.

That afternoon when I got to my locker, somebody had scrawled "Mormon" across the door, and then that same somebody or somebody else had crossed out the second *M* so that it read *Moron.* So much for making a good impression for the Church. Even Lexie treated me with something resembling contempt. It bothered me more when she treated Arnold the same way. He'd had nothing to do with what had happened.

Some friends of Abe Stanley's who'd started eating lunch at our table a week or two before the Christmas break didn't come back after the break, opting instead for a table at the far end of the cafeteria with some guys on the soccer team. Parry and Abe had been hanging out with Tanny and Tallulah and their friends, and they joined the thespian group table, once in a while at first, and then daily. That left me with Beezer and somebody named Farwell who had plastered-down hair and an attitude. He mellowed somewhat when I helped him figure out his algebra.

Arnold had said he was trying to switch to my lunch, and I hoped he would. I knew I had his support and probably always would. I had my family's support as well. Soon after the Kalamazoo reception, I'd finally told my parents everything that had been going on.

"Oh my gosh, Kenny," my mother said. "Why on earth didn't you talk to us and tell us you were going through all this?"

"You had plenty to worry about with the wedding," I said.

"You could still have come to us. No matter how busy we are or seem to be, we're never too busy to talk to you about your problems."

Dad, as quick on the spiritual draw as ever, asked me if I wanted a blessing. I said I did, and felt comfort and relief when he pressed his hands on my head and blessed me with courage and the ability to stand alone if necessary for what I believed was right. He blessed me that I would make it through this difficult period. "Thanks, Dad," I told him. "I needed that." And I did. There are some things you just don't know if you can get through by yourself.

⊚

Well, "making it through" was what I ended up doing. Each day I got up, got dressed, and went to school. Each afternoon I entered invoices into the computer and then spent the rest of the evening studying for classes and finishing up papers, stopping only for dinner. Every night I prayed harder than I'd prayed ever before for strength and for Alysse—that she'd get reinstated and that everything would work out for her after graduation.

After a while something came into my mind that seemed to stay there and build a nest. *There are people out there in the world in a lot worse shape than you are,* I could almost hear. *Gird up your loins.* Something else came through even more powerfully: *Christ suffered for us all, including you—and including Alysse.*

Two days before the end of the semester, I realized I should have been praying for Arnold as well when I came around the corner and saw some members of the hockey club grabbing at his hat. He put up a good fight, but by the time I caught up, the smallest and apparently the quickest of the group was running off with it.

"It's okay," Arnold said. "I'll get it back . . . eventually."

In Spanish Alysse remained polite but aloof. It's hard to explain how sad I felt that things had become awkward between us. She still joked with others, but not with me. I thought at the time it was because she'd had a chance to review everything and had decided she had good reason to be angry with me. It wasn't until later that I realized she was maybe just embarrassed.

And then the semester was over. No longer did I have two classes with Allyson Pringle. Even though history was a full year course, Alysse transferred to Mrs. Petrie's class. And who could blame her? I stuck with Thorndike, even though I had a hard time even looking at the guy. I knew I would need to forgive him, but again, it was going to be hard. As far as Spanish was concerned, I'd promised Dad that I'd sign up for accounting, and the only time it was taught was third period. The family business was going better, thanks to out-of-state sales, and I needed to pick up a few more bookkeeping skills. I had no choice but to transfer to Alvarez's fifth period. So now I had *no* classes with Alysse. I still heard things about her, of course. Arnold and his sisters and people in my classes still talked and laughed about her antics. She apparently hadn't let her setback get her down too much. At least, she acted like it hadn't. If anything, she was in better comic form than ever.

Parry, who landed the part of the rejected boyfriend, Hugo Peabody, in *Bye Bye Birdie,* let me know one night when we both hitched a ride with Arnold that Alysse *had* tried out for the part of Mama Peterson, just as she and I had talked about. He said that although Mrs. Dallask hadn't officially given it to her, she'd unofficially told Alysse she could have the part after the air cleared a little. In fact, because Alysse was still on probation, the teacher asked the cast members not to advertise the fact that Alysse was coming to rehearsals. The star role of Kim MacAffee went to an unknown junior, Mitzi McCormick, who'd come out of nowhere to beat out Tallulah and Dee Dee, among others.

"Who's playing Albert Peterson?" I asked.

"Carlin Stevens," said Parry, "but he won't be tap-dancing."

I nodded. "And is Tyrone playing Conrad Birdie?"

"Good guess."

I was glad Alysse had landed the part she wanted, or that it looked like she would be playing Mama Peterson, but I also worried that if she got too busy with the play she wouldn't have the time necessary to meet the requirements to get back into her school office.

In orchestra, Mr. Hammond told us we wouldn't be practicing with the cast members until the final two rehearsals. We'd started working on "Honestly Sincere" and "Put On a Happy Face" right after the break and soon had those numbers down well enough to perfect a couple more. I practiced extra hard, maybe hoping that by the time the orchestra got together with the cast, Alysse would be so impressed at my skill on the trombone that she'd want to be my friend again. Of course, I wasn't counting on it.

By the second week in the new semester, I was pretty much a nonentity at our school again. Well, almost. I'd been debating whether to stick with the peer tutoring program. When I was assigned a couple of refugees from Zimbabwe, I decided to go ahead. I doubted they'd be all that concerned about my status at the school.

Three weeks into the semester, a girl in orchestra named Amy Washburn, one of the flutists, sent word through Beezer that she wanted to get to know me better. I figured that either she was one of those free spirits who didn't care what others thought, or the animosity toward me was fading. Amy was a cute, nice girl, and I was civil and everything, but I just really wasn't interested.

Ren wasted no time moving in on Alysse again. Possibly because he didn't want to risk alienating her, he left me alone. He even seemed to be joking around with people he would never have associated with earlier in the year. I hoped he really was changing and that it wasn't just an act this time.

Arnold and I had basically traded lunches, but Beezer and

Farwell still had my same lunch and soon a couple of Farwell's friends joined us: Del Riddle and Ben Gallante. It was obvious by Del's floral shirt and Ben's interesting cap that they were creative spirits who didn't care what people thought. Even though we didn't have a lot in common, they were nice enough to me and I returned the favor.

It was Ben who told me about the big party Ren had hosted the previous Sunday night. "Booze flowing like the Rhine," Del added. "Other stuff too. Then here come the politzei."

"The police?" I said, looking up, from my sandwich.

"Oh yeah. A big bust. I heard April McKuen talking about it."

My next question, said quietly and with concern, was, "Did she say anything about Alysse Pringle being there?"

"Somebody said that Alysse and some of her friends, Dee Dee Smit for one, left early and were out of there by the time everything fell apart. But Caleb Sweeney got nabbed."

I remembered what a good sport Caleb had been the night of the dance, and his funny and pious expression when Dee Dee had placed that halo on his head. I felt bad for him.

"They're saying Ren will probably only get a slap on the wrist," lisped Ben. "His father's on the city council. You watch, somebody else will end up the scapegoat."

Sure enough, the next day, Caleb, who'd checked into my accounting class just a few days before, wasn't in school. I heard from Abe that the powers that be had come down hard on him and he wouldn't be returning that year or graduating with us. Ren, however, was laughing and visiting and joking in the front hall with Alysse and some others that same day, acting like nothing whatsoever was wrong. After school he was sitting on the stairs in the exact place I'd occupied for a while. And he was there again the following day. But Alysse wasn't.

It was a relief to me when I didn't see Alysse with Ren all that week. A few weeks later I heard that Alysse was going to the Spring Formal with Carlin Stevens. Carlin was a good guy and I was happy for them. At least, I told myself I was.

Ren was soon strutting around the school with a junior whose skirt barely made it over her behind. Next thing we knew, Ren had taken up smoking. I felt kind of sorry for him. Ren had taken a nosedive in acceptance just like I had, but for different reasons. I felt a little less sorry for him, however, when he cornered me in the school basement and slammed me against the lockers. "You don't have Alysse to protect you now, do you?" Nate came around the corner right then, as if it had all been planned out. His surprise punch in the stomach knocked the wind out of me. But I was bigger than I'd been in junior high, and I think they were aware of that, so it was basically a hit-and-run.

Other than that episode, things seemed to be going a little better for me. Time has a way of easing problems. I had an hour here and there when I was able not to think about what had happened with Alysse. You move on because life continues and because you don't have much of a choice. After the big party scandal, people stopped making comments and giving me dirty looks. I guess just about everything gets old, and they had new and more exciting things to talk about. Still, it was a happy day for me when Alysse was reinstated as a student body officer. I still remember the exact date: April 10th. It wasn't long before the next elections, but I was still thrilled and relieved. I really wanted to congratulate her by e-mail, text her, or maybe even call her, but by that time, we hadn't talked for so long that I couldn't bring myself to push the keys.

Gradually, life pretty much went back to how it had been before I'd become good friends with Alysse—boring, in other words. I decided it was just as well, and I began thinking ahead to graduation and to my mission. But it wasn't like I could just wipe the memories of Alysse and her friendship from my life. I still saw her in the halls off and on, and she had a chance to conduct another couple of events.

On days when I didn't see her, I was hearing about her. Students were really looking forward to the play, and there were nice-looking posters all over the school that somebody said Charlotte had designed. I was looking forward not only to the play itself but also to those last two rehearsals when the orchestra would be joining the rest of the performers. "It's gonna be a good one," Parry let me know.

Things became a little more exciting for me when my balsa bridge science project went on to region, where it got an award for excellence. Then several teachers nominated me for the "Student Academic and Community Service Award" sponsored by the newspaper. Alysse was voted "Most Caring Student Leader" by Hollenda students, and "Top Drama Student" as well. There were rumors that a talent scout was coming to Kalamazoo just to see our play.

And then on a Monday morning a few days before the play, I heard something that sucked the air right out of me. Janette Osborne told me the unbelievably bad news in first period.

Chapter Twenty-Five

I'm surprised you didn't know. I thought you and Alysse were good friends," Janette said. She'd been out of school with mono for almost two months and had apparently missed more than just school work.

"I haven't talked to Alysse too much this semester," I finally managed to choke out. I wasn't about to explain, not right then. "I can't believe it. Are you sure that really happened? Are you sure her brother was actually killed?"

"Oh, yeah. It's all around the school. It happened Saturday."

I shook my head and exhaled slowly as I remembered the happy look on Allyson's face, the lilt in her voice whenever she'd talked about Pete. "She was really close to him," I told Janette.

Janette nodded, her mouth pulled down. "That's what I heard."

"Do you know any more?"

"Just that it was some freak accident that happened when he

was on his way to the library at his college. He goes—I should say he *went*—to some Ivy League school, Harvard or something."

"Yale," I said. "Alysse said he went to Yale. She was really proud of him."

Mrs. Cavanaugh had been deployed and wasn't teaching that semester, and her substitute for the remainder of the year had already pulled out her binder and looked like she was ready to get started. "School isn't over yet, students," she reminded us. "We do have a few more weeks." I was glad I had a reason to turn to the front of the classroom.

For the remaining forty-five minutes I just sat there staring straight ahead, kneading my hands, aware that our teacher's lips were moving but not hearing actual words. I couldn't stop thinking about Alysse and how she had to be feeling. For an instant or two I found myself imagining how I would feel if something happened to my brother or one of my sisters—especially Monica. It had been hard enough having her go away to school, and even harder when she got married. The thought of her suddenly not being here on earth anymore was too painful to entertain. Even with the gospel and what I knew, just thinking about losing one of my family members hurt so badly that I had to leave that place in my mind. My throat felt tight and my whole face stiffened as I realized that for Alysse this wasn't imaginary or some mental scene she could click off. This was real. How was she going to cope? It was clear she didn't have the best support system at home. Even worse, she didn't have the gospel of Jesus Christ in her life to comfort her. It had been Pete who'd been her main support, and now he was gone. How was she going to make it through this?

181

Arnold had driven home with some of the band members, but he stopped by my house afterwards. I was still out on the porch when he quietly joined me. My friend respectfully took off his new, even better, Australian outback hat. "Pretty awful about Alysse's brother, huh?" he said quietly.

"It sure is," I answered, barely moving. He didn't say much else, but sat on the edge of the green metal chair across from me for quite a while even though it was really cold again.

"Are you going to do anything? Call her or anything?" he finally asked.

"I really don't know if she'd want to hear from me," I answered. "We haven't talked for a long time, and we're not really what you'd call friends anymore. Not since . . . well, you know. I guess I *could* send a card or something."

"I'll bet she'd appreciate that," Arnold said.

"You think she would?"

"Sure, wouldn't anybody?"

I nodded slowly, and as I thought again about how I might feel in Allyson's place, I realized that knowing people cared would definitely help. "Maybe I *will* run over to the drugstore and find a card. Do you wanna come?"

"If you need me to," Arnold said. "What I should really do is get home and catch up on geometry homework. That is, if I want to graduate." Arnold had a bad habit of avoiding homework until the last possible minute. If he said he needed to get home and do geometry, it probably meant it was an emergency. But I was in no position to be judgmental. I'd had my own struggles with time management there for a while.

"I think I can handle it," I let him know.

"K, my mate, good luck." He picked up his hat. His eyebrows and mouth were pressed forward, his hair flat against his head for a change. Arnold's face had filled out a little during the past school year and, like me, he'd bulked up some in the previous few months.

"Thanks." I smiled and slapped his palm listlessly.

After he'd chugged away in the old Pontiac, I didn't move, but stayed on the porch until Mom came out. "Don't you think you'd better come in now?" she asked gently. "It's a little cold to be sitting out here." She was right. It had been springlike earlier in the week, but now winter had come back with a solid right jab, as if letting us know it wasn't going to go quietly. I pulled myself off the swing and followed her into the house. "Do you want some hot chocolate, honey?" Mom had heard about what had happened through a woman in her book group whose son had graduated the same year as Pete.

"I'm thinking I might run to the drugstore and get a card."

"That's a good idea, but don't you want to get warm first?"

"I'm okay."

"Well, maybe getting Alysse a card will help you both feel a little better."

It would take more than a card, I thought, but I nodded numbly as I pulled the van keys from the hook in the hall, my jacket on my shoulder where Mom had thrown it. But then I just stood there swinging the keys. I guess Mom realized she was hovering, so she left for the kitchen. After several minutes, I hung the keys carefully back on the hook. "Never mind," I called out.

"You're not going now?"

"No."

Mom came to the door. "Why not?"

I shrugged. "I'm not sure."

I passed her and went into the kitchen, where I sat on one of the wooden chairs by the table. Finally I took a sip of the hot chocolate my mom had poured for me, holding the cup with both hands as I tried to answer the question myself. I knew part of the reason I wasn't taking over a card was because I wasn't sure I'd know what to say to Alysse when I gave it to her. It had been a few days since the accident, and it felt too late to *mail* a card. The bigger concern was whether Alysse would even want to hear from a person who'd made life so much harder for her during her senior year. I was afraid my showing up with a card would make her feel worse than she was already feeling. "We're really not friends anymore," I told my mother.

"Of course you are. You're friends with everyone." It was a mother thing to say.

The next day I heard from several sources that Alysse still wasn't in school. After school, I almost changed my mind again about the card and thought about stopping at Walgreens, but I didn't.

Alysse wasn't in school that next day either. In orchestra, Jake Huong was talking with Amy about the accident when I came into class. "They're not sure if he fell asleep or what happened. Maybe he was high on something."

"I don't think he would have been high on something," I butted in. "Alysse said he was a sensible guy."

Jake changed course then and started talking about the play, which was scheduled for the weekend. "Everybody's wondering if Alysse will be able to pull off *Bye Bye Birdie* now. I heard Julie Felix is practicing the backup, just in case. But I heard Alysse was kind of the assistant director, too, and was helping everybody with their parts."

I remembered then that Parry had told me the same thing. Even though her own part wasn't huge, Alysse had been playing a major role in pulling others along and encouraging cast members to really put it all out there.

Jake's bringing up the play reminded me again that the orchestra was scheduled to rehearse with the cast members that very night. Mr. Hammond had only reminded us a few hundred times. In fact, as soon as he called us to attention, he reminded us again. With all that had happened, I'd forgotten completely. The big one, the dress rehearsal, was scheduled for the following day—Thursday.

Chapter Twenty-Six

Before we started the rehearsal that night, Mrs. Dallask gathered the performers together. "As most of you have probably heard by now, Allyson Pringle had a death in her family—her brother. I imagine you're wondering if she'll still be participating with us, and I don't think anyone knows that right now. I'm really not sure if Allyson knows herself. But even if Allyson doesn't feel she can perform, I think she'd want the rest of us to do the best job we can. I think Allyson would want us to knock 'em dead." Mrs. Dallask paused for a split second and blinked a few times, as if concerned about that particular choice of words. She opened her mouth, shut it, then opened it again to continue: "Anyway, before we get started today, I have a sympathy card here that any of you are welcome to sign, if you'd like to, and if anyone would like to contribute to flowers, I'll send an envelope around as well. At least, I hope that isn't against school policy. If it is, I guess I'll be giving you the money back."

"What if one of us collects? What if I collect?" said Mitzi, stepping in. "If it's a student's idea to do it, then there shouldn't be any trouble about it because they won't be able to say anyone was pressured by the school or anything." Mitzi was apparently more street smart than she looked. Mrs. Dallask seemed to recognize the wisdom in Mitzi's suggestion and readily went along.

As the card and envelope were passed from one person to the next, I saw kids open their wallets without any hesitation and pull out bills. I put in a five myself, all I had, but it still didn't seem enough.

After rehearsal, I once again thought about stopping by the drugstore for a card. Just a card and even flowers with a large group seemed too impersonal. But it had been several days now. Maybe it was already too late to even drop a card off. And again, would Alysse even want to hear from me?

But on the way home, I put myself in Allyson's place one more time. As I thought about how I would feel if something happened to Kip or Lynette or Monica, I realized that losing such a close family member would completely dwarf just about anything else that had ever happened to me. It occurred to me that Alysse probably didn't care anymore about what had happened at the end of first semester. Even being relieved of her school office for a while, as awful as it had seemed at the time, wouldn't be all that significant in comparison to what she was dealing with now. I realized as well that it probably would never be too late to let her know somebody cared. Losing her brother would be impacting her for a very long time—her entire life.

"Mom, I'm going to the drugstore," I called out as I stepped in the door. "This time I'm really going."

"Okay, Kendall."

◎

It was much warmer than it had been the night before, and the snow had pretty much melted. Walgreens was just around the corner from our house and west a couple of blocks, close enough to cycle. I pulled my bike out from behind some bins in the garage, checked the tires, and then headed down Wilshire.

It was obvious by the huge bin of colored baskets in the front of the store that Easter was on its way. Several giant Easter baskets on the aisle end were stuffed with toys and candy, and I could make out a bucket and shovel in one of them. Not that many years before I would have been salivating at the sight of such a big basket stuffed with cheap toys. There's something about cellophane. But now I headed straight past it down the aisle to the cards, barely glancing at the jelly beans, chocolate bunnies, and so forth crammed into the shelves.

In the past I'd found some fairly decent cards for birthdays and holidays at this store, but this time as I pulled out one card after another I couldn't find anything at all that seemed right. One sympathy card had a picture of a cross and rosary on the front—another was far too fancy and glittery looking. None of the messages even came close to capturing what I wanted to say. Not that I knew what I wanted to say. Finally, I moved to the blank card section and found a card with a painting by Monet—the one with the bridge. Girls seemed to like Monet paintings, at least my sisters both did, and I pulled it out and took it to the register.

Back home I couldn't bring myself to open the card, and it wasn't until almost eight that I finally found a pen and wrote, "I was sorry to hear about your brother." Then I signed my name and stuck it into the envelope. But I didn't seal it. A few seconds later, I pulled the card out again, feeling strongly that I needed to say something more. I stuck my pen in my mouth and studied the watercolor print of some apples on our kitchen wall. Alysse, as far as I knew, wasn't at all religious, but at a time like this . . . what could I say that would help her feel better? I said a silent prayer and then, digging deep, wrote a few words that I hoped were inspired. I sealed the envelope, let my mother know my plans to drop the card off, and found the van keys.

After I pulled up in front of Allyson's midsized, fairly upscale rambler about ten minutes later, I stayed in the van for quite a while trying to muster up some courage. Finally, I opened the van door, climbed up the nice cobblestone stairs to a rich-looking front door, and tapped the copper knocker against it.

The sleekly dressed older woman in a navy jacket and checked pants who answered the door looked a little old to be Allyson's stepmother.

"I go to school with Allyson," I said. "I heard about her brother and, umm . . ." I didn't know if this woman was a relative, but just in case, I said, "I'm sorry about your family's loss." The words seemed small and stupid and meaningless. "Could you please give Allyson this card?"

"Thank you," said the woman politely. "I'm Allyson's

step-grandmother and I'll make sure she gets this. And your name
is . . . ?"

"Kendall Archer."

"Well, thank you, Kendall. You're very kind." She remained formal. "Goodness, it's getting dark out here already."

"Yes it is." I couldn't think of anything more to say, and I took
a step back. "S'okay, anyway, thanks." My knee buckled as I turned,
but I caught myself and made it back to our van, where I hurriedly
shut the door. But even after I slid back into the front seat, I just
sat there staring straight ahead. Finally I turned the key in the ignition, flipped on the lights, and stepped on the gas pedal. Instead of
heading straight, however, I turned in the direction of the school,
pulled onto Autumn Street, and then headed into the park. Inside,
I followed the inner park road until I got to the baseball field
where I'd played Little League. In the distance was the outfield
where just about every year I was assigned to right field and where
I'd made a few catches, but missed the rest. It was getting dark and
I could hardly see the field but I stared in that direction anyway.
Finally, I hit the dashboard. A card? A stupid card. Why hadn't I
done more? Was that really all my friendship with Alysse was
worth to me? Why did I have to be such an insecure idiot? I should
have taken flowers on my own—done *something*. A card didn't
seem anywhere near enough. *Life stinks*, I thought. And then, I did
something I rarely do. I swore under my breath.

Chapter Twenty-Seven

That next day, Thursday, Alysse was back in school in her standard red glasses and carrying her Minnie Mouse bag. She was wearing a neon green shirt with bright pink flamingos printed on it. When I caught a glimpse of her from half a hall away, my insides leaped. By second period everybody in the school seemed to know she was back.

"Maybe this means she'll be in the play," Carolee Pruitt, who had a bit part in the fainting scene, speculated. "Cross your fingers."

All day long I wondered if Alysse would show up at the dress rehearsal. I polished my trombone during lunch and went into the rest room to practice a few measures from the introduction. I wasn't quite warmed up and consequently played the same few notes several times in a row. "Man, I thought someone had a real problem," a guy with a big tattoo of a spider on his forearm said when he came out of one of the stalls.

After school I stayed in the orchestra room and practiced again, working on a section of "One Boy." Then I hurried to the auditorium. I headed straight to the pit, but not before I spotted Alysse up on the stage.

"Yeeees, she's gonna do it," one of our violinists whispered excitedly. In fact, everyone seemed to be whispering about the fact that Alysse was there, yet nobody said anything to Alysse herself. When Alysse called out something to Tyrone, a crack about his costume, kids finally relaxed and started joking with her.

Because Alysse *was* there, the dress rehearsal went far better than the rehearsal the night before had gone. And when it was her turn, Alysse performed her lines flawlessly—even the longest portion, where Mama Peterson tells her son that it's confirmed she has a "condition," and that one thing doctors can't cure is a "condition."

"Aaalbert!" she screeched out a line or two later. I thought Alysse captured the role even better than either actress in the movie versions had. Cast members, including orchestra members, applauded, cheered, and hooted at her.

We'd been instructed not to stop for any reason during this rehearsal, but Mrs. Dallask, still laughing, broke her own rule and said, "Sorry, I can't help it. I need to tell you, Allyson, that was wonderful. Thank you for your courage."

Alysse bowed and smiled. "I didn't bring all my costume. I'll have it ready by tomorrow."

"That would be perfect." Mrs. Dallask looked stage right. "Okay, Act Three. No more stops." A few scenes later, our dress rehearsal was over and I was playing my trombone with emotion and full power during the finale.

"Excellent, excellent job," said Mrs. Dallask, a ring of excitement in her voice. She clapped her hands together. "Folks, I think we've got a hit on our hands! Now, remember to be here by six P.M. sharp tomorrow. I'll say it again: Excellent! Bravo! Good work!"

While a few orchestra members visited with cast members, and others congregated in the far section of the pit, I opted to get my trombone put away and was busy adjusting the mouthpiece when I sensed someone directly above me. Glancing up, I saw that it was Alysse looking down at me. "Oh, hi," I said, jerking up.

Supporting herself with one hand, she lowered herself to the stage floor. "I . . . umm . . . wondered if I could talk to you about something."

I grabbed my music. "Sure, right now?"

"No, it's too late now. I need to get home and you probably do too." She lifted her eyebrows and tried to smile. "Homework, right?"

I nodded.

Her smile evaporated. "How about tomorrow right after school?"

"Sure, yeah—sure. Where?"

"I'll meet you at the big oak next to the gym building."

"We're on."

I was still nodding when Jake, who was waiting for friends, called to her. "Whooo, Alysse, you make one hot old Mama."

"Well, you look like an old bag yourself, hotshot!" she called back.

Jake chortled; Tyrone did an Elvis hip thrust, Mitzi snorted; and several others hooted once again, obviously relieved to have good old Alysse back.

But when Alysse turned toward me, her eyes were serious again. "The big oak," she repeated almost fiercely. "I'll see you there."

"I'll be there," I said. *Double promise.*

The next afternoon after school I got out of seventh period plenty fast enough, but then I just couldn't seem to get out the school door. First Mrs. Bertrand, my physics teacher, cornered me in the hall. She'd nominated me to the newspaper's academic awards and wanted to talk to me about my portfolio. She was ecstatic that I'd been able to raise my score on the ACT two points the final time I had taken it. "Excuse me, ma'am, but I have an appointment," I said when I finally got a word in.

"Oh, yes, yes, go right ahead," said Mrs. Bertrand. "I'll talk to you tomorrow after class." She was rubbing her hands together as she walked away.

When I got to my locker, Arnold wanted to tell me all about what had happened in band. Trumpet player A had broken the nose of trumpet player B when he'd "accidentally" smacked him with his horn. Since both musicians liked the same flag twirler, the circumstances looked suspicious. "You know what?" I interrupted Arnold. "I'm gonna have to hear this later. I've got to get out of here. I've got to meet somebody."

Arnold's eyebrows popped up. "Who? What's going on, bloke?"

"I'll tell you later." As I pulled around him and hurried down the hall, I could feel his eyes on my back.

When I saw Mrs. Carru coming toward me, I quickly flipped a right turn and hurried to the closest exit. Even though I owed the woman big-time, I couldn't afford to have her stop me to chat as well. But it wasn't the best door to go out, and I was out of breath by the time I got around the far corner of the school.

At first I didn't see Alysse. "Oh, maaaan!" I sighed. I swung my arms over my head, thinking that because I had taken so long to get all the way around the school, she'd given up on me. *I should have grabbed my phone from my car,* I chastised myself. *I could have let her know I would be a few minutes.* I had walked right past the parking lot. Now I was sure I'd missed her.

But then the Beal twins, who were walking their bicycles past the tree, stopped and waved at someone behind it. When they laughed heartily at the person's response, and one of them moved her cycle forward and called something in that direction, I moved slightly to my left a ways, hopeful. Sure enough, after several steps I spotted the edge of the familiar Minnie Mouse book bag and the tip of a bright yellow tennis shoe. Alysse was still there!

"Hi," I said quietly when I reached her. "Sorry it took me so long. I was afraid you'd left. You wanna talk here, or should we go somewhere?"

Alysse flashed me the required smile. "I think I'd rather we got out of here. Do you mind?"

"Not at all. How about the park?"

"You're on. We can take my car; I'm really close."

"And your car probably runs. You never know with mine," I said, trying to joke. Actually, the van had been running fairly well since we got it tuned up. I wasn't sure I was glad about that, but it was just as well, since the wedding had eaten up our new-car money.

As we came out from behind the tree, a jeep swung by, honking, with Dee Dee Smit practically falling out of it. Alysse lifted her fingers into a V. "Do you mind driving?" she asked quietly, as she grinned and waved at someone in a Camry.

"You sure?"

"Yeah, I'd rather you drove." She pulled the keys out of her bag and pushed the unlock button, then handed them to me, the car key extended.

In a few minutes, I was backing her Ford Fusion out of her parking stall. I carefully pulled through the school lot as Alysse continued waving at people, giving herself rabbit ears, lifting her thumb, smiling and nodding. We'd barely hit Pine Avenue when Tyrone Brown and some of his friends started following us, honking loudly.

"Why don't you turn left here?" Alysse said. "Maybe we can lose them."

"Okay."

The turning lane was clear and I carefully pulled in, just making the arrow. Had this been a movie chase scene, Tyrone would have screeched from his lane to ours and followed on our tail, sparks flying. But since there was a truck that had turned into the lane before him and a car right behind him, he and his friends just honked one last time, waved, and headed straight.

A block later I turned right, then drove west on Maddington until we got to the park on Autumn Street that I'd visited just two nights before. I pulled into a parking stall and turned off the ignition.

After all that honking and traffic, it seemed really quiet. Alysse took a deep breath as she stared out the passenger window. "You wanna get out?" I asked.

"Sure, why don't we get out and walk around a little bit?"

A minute or two later we were walking along the lane by the duck pond toward the picnic area on the opposite side of the ball fields. It had rained earlier, but had cleared up since, and there was still a little moisture in the air. At least it wasn't cold. Like I said, you never know in April, and we were lucky it wasn't storming. "Sorry to put you to this trouble," Alysse said. "I'm sure you have better things to do." Her voice sounded like it was coming from a cavern inside her.

"It's no trouble at all. Is this area okay?"

"Maybe over there. It's more secluded," she said, pointing toward a section with trees. As we headed toward them to some tables and a bench, Alysse kept her eyes on the ground. I couldn't see her face because of her hair, but then she sniffed, and a tear dripped down to the grass.

Grateful that my mother always made sure family members were supplied with tissue packets, I reached into the pocket of my jacket and handed her the entire packet.

"Thanks. Sorry." Alysse pulled out a tissue and wiped her eyes.

As we sat down on the bench, Alysse pushed the tissue against one eye and then the other.

"I appreciate your driving us here," she said. "I needed to get away from school." She paused and inhaled. "Everybody there expects me to joke around, and it's not all that easy being funny all the time. It's a lot of pressure." She laughed a little. "That sounds weird, doesn't it?" Alysse pulled the tissue down to her nose, sniffed, pushed back some strands of her hair, and glanced up long enough for me to see that her eyes were trimmed in red.

"I think I understand what you're saying."

She stared down at the hand not gripping the tissues, and stretched her delicate fingers. It was easy to forget how small-boned she was. Finally she looked up. "You're actually one of the few people who sees me as more than just funny. The problem is that a person doesn't always *feel* like being funny. Like today. I didn't feel like joking around, but nobody knows how to react to an unfunny Alysse." She sniffed again. "But it's like I'm letting people down if I don't play my usual role." Her bottom lip began to tremble, and she pulled it in and scraped over it with her top teeth. "You know what they say: the show must go on." I knew she wasn't just talking about the play.

"You go ahead and cry if you need to, Alysse," I said. "I don't mind at all. I can handle that just fine."

"You . . . I . . ." It was as if my making that statement gave her permission to unleash the tears, and sure enough, Allyson's shoulders and back started jerking up and down. I felt helpless and inadequate. "I'm sorry," she said with a swallow. "I feel so stupid. I'm so sorry."

"No, it's fine." I put my hand on hers and pressed gently. "It's totally all right. You're among friends."

Alysse hiccupped, half laughed, then hiccupped again. "Okay," she said as she struggled to regain control of herself. "Okey-dokey!" She laughed nervously again, took a deep breath, and tried to smile. "So, I suppose you're wondering why I called this little meeting, huh?" But then she turned serious again. "Well, I'll tell you." Her chin was trembling now. "It was that card you gave me." Alysse drew in a deep breath. "You said something on it that I memorized. You said . . ." She paused and swallowed again. "You said, 'I have strong faith that Pete still lives.'"

Alysse pulled in her bottom lip and then began whispering hoarsely. "I've got to know more about that. Nobody in my family has ever been very religious. I'm not sure why. Pete was the closest to being religious. He actually went to church a few times—the Lutheran, I think it was, or maybe the Methodist." She was losing control again and paused once more. "I've never really even thought about any of it that much—religion, I mean—spiritual things. But now I really need to know." She half snorted. "I don't think I can get through this if I don't. I just . . . I need to know where Pete is right now." Alysse pressed the back of her hand against her mouth and looked into my eyes, then down again quickly. "That's why I wanted to talk to you." After a few seconds she managed to grin and punch me in the arm. "Let me put it this way, hombre: If you say something is true, then I can believe it." She laughed a little. "Because you've got to be the doggoned most honest person I've ever met." Alysse turned serious again. "And I know I can trust you, Kendall."

Now I felt *my* bottom lip begin to shake. "I'm glad you feel that way, Alysse," I said softly but emphatically. "I'm really glad because I meant what I said on my card." I tapped my chest. "I believe—in fact, I know, right in here, right down to my core, that your brother is in a good place." This time I sniffed. "And I'd be glad to tell you more." Now I felt my eyes beginning to well up, because I really did have so much to tell her about the Restoration and families being together and about Christ's Resurrection and Atonement that made it possible for us not only to be with our loved ones but with Christ and our Father in Heaven someday. There was a lot to cover, yet I wanted to keep it simple so as not to overwhelm her. I knew one thing for sure: I would really need to rely on the Spirit to guide me through it all. In the meantime, old Kendall-Wendall was struggling himself to keep control. I cleared my throat and sniffed again. "But first, could I borrow back some of those tissues?" I asked. "It looks like I might be needing them before our little meeting is over."

Chapter Twenty-Eight

That night in our school play, Allyson Pringle, jester of Hollenda High, put on the performance of her life. The instant she tromped on the stage wearing an old house-dress, ugly hiking boots, and a small hat perched atop a raggedy wig, the audience went crazy. I was laughing so hard from the orchestra pit that I was fearful I wouldn't have enough air left when it came time to play the numbers that followed.

In the finale, people jumped up, lifted their hands, and cheered for all the performers, especially the main stars, but most of all for Alysse. "Pringle! Pringle!" they shouted.

It was pretty much the same scenario at the matinee perform-ance on Saturday, and again Saturday night. In fact, Mitzi and Parry and Carlin and Tyrone, the leads, graciously stepped back to give Alysse center stage.

At the party afterwards, I wanted to congratulate Alysse in per-son, tell her how great she'd done, but she was surrounded by fans all evening. Our eyes did meet at one point, and she smiled and lifted her chin at me, but then several more people rushed in.

Since Alysse wasn't in any of my classes that semester, and since things got pretty crazy those last few weeks of school, we didn't talk again. Oh, we said hi to each other, but that was about it. Generally, she was with people again, laughing and joking. That was okay because I was busy myself, getting ready for my interview with the judges for the academic awards finals—which, by the way, I didn't even come close to winning. It wasn't that many weeks later that I got my mission call to the Brazil Porto Alegre North Mission and was informed there would be no flight to Provo because Brazil had its own Missionary Training Center. You learn your geography when you get a mission call, and our globe showed that Brazil was far bigger than I'd realized, and a long, long way from Kalamazoo. I was excited, yes, but also scared spitless.

Alysse, I heard from good sources, left not long after graduation for New York, where she planned to start school in the fall. She'd been accepted into a decent performing arts school, according to Parry's girlfriend, Tanny. I was relieved and happy for Alysse. I asked Tanny to give me her address as soon as she got it. I didn't tell her it was because I planned to have the missionaries in New York look her up. But then Tanny headed for the British Isles with Rhonda and Dee Dee and Tallulah. I heard through the grapevine that Allyson's father and his new wife and kids had moved to Connecticut, so I couldn't even go that route.

I didn't try to squeeze in any college myself but worked full-time for my father all summer and almost all of September and part of October. I wanted to do everything I could to get the finance end of his business completely updated and organized for him. I left clear instructions for Dad on how to get where he needed to be on the computer. Time went fast, and the next thing I knew I was on that plane.

I'd only been out a couple of months when I found myself dealing with some pretty major knee issues. It's amazing how fast a little problem can magnify when you agitate it on a daily basis. It ticked me off that, as bad as I was at sports, those few games I'd played at church and in our driveway would affect me to the extent they had. That was what I got for trying to keep up with my brother. I knew within just a few weeks of being out in the field that it had been a big mistake not to get a relatively minor knee problem taken care of before I left. Not telling my doctor or even my parents about it had been just plain dumb. Soon I was paying the price.

I have to say that I lasted as long as I possibly could, constantly telling myself my knee wasn't hurting as bad as it was. I did talk to a doctor who was president of one of the branches and followed some suggestions he gave me. I thought that with time, my knee would heal itself. But it had other ideas. Four and a half months into my mission it completely refused to cooperate. Basically, it went on strike, which meant my whole leg had no choice but to go on strike along with it. In other words, I couldn't walk. Five months after I'd entered the mission field I was on a plane again— heading right back to the states, Michigan, and home.

Those next few weeks after my surgery, I was one distraught elder. Even though it was wonderful to see my family, I felt like an unregistered foreigner. I wasn't supposed to be here at my house in Kalamazoo! I was in the middle of my mission! I worried about what was going on out in the mission office and hoped that who-ever was subbing for me wasn't messing up the system I'd set up. I missed President and Sister Phillips and the other missionaries in my mission terribly and wondered what was happening with the DaSilva family and Barreto Marinetzo, people that my companion and I had been teaching in the evenings. I needed to get back! But recovery was far harder than I'd anticipated and I wasn't exactly doing laps even a month later.

I have to say, I did get some genuine comic relief when Arnold got his mission call. That was something to witness. Arnold raced all the way to my house and rushed in, shouting: "I'm going to Australia! I'm going to Australia! Perth! Perth, Australia!"

He threw his outback hat into the air, caught it on his head, then pulled it off again and twirled it as he danced.

I was as amazed as he was. "How'd you do that? You got con-nections or something? Man, you must live right! Hey, you even have a head start in the language!"

"Can you believe it!? Can you believe it? Australia!" he kept shouting. At several points, he leaped even higher than I ever had.

"Watch your knees," I warned him.

Arnold's amazing news kept me going for several days, but soon he was busy getting everything together for his mission, and I was back at my job of being patient. I kept up on my scripture study and spoke Portuguese to Mom and Dad, my grandparents, my brothers and sisters, their babies, and even Lucky Duck. I continued praying in Portuguese as well.

Then I got the bad news: I wouldn't be going back to Brazil. The Church's reassignment committee sent me a letter saying it had been determined that I should go to an area where I'd have easier access to medical help and to a car. Now I was as upset for myself as I'd been happy for Arnold. In fact, I decided to plunge into a slump and wallow there. Why was this happening? I wanted to go back to Brazil! I belonged in Brazil. I'd prayed like crazy to get better so I could get back there. It wasn't fair!

Those days following my reassignment notice to California, I lay around in my room downstairs with only Lucky Duck as company. "Don't you need to do your exercise therapy?" Mom kept asking.

It was a Saturday when Mom brought in the mail and handed me an envelope. She raised and lowered her eyebrows twice. "This one's from New York."

I didn't open the card immediately. I just studied the envelope carefully; it had a return address but no name. The handwriting was large, but I didn't dare hope it was from Alysse. Then again, who else did I know in New York?

Fearful of being disappointed, I finally opened the letter slowly, making sure I got just the envelope. Then I flipped open the card. "Hey, Archer!" I read. "You arched your arrow right into my heart!" I read on . . ."so when the guys on bicycles stopped near my apartment in Manhattan, what could I do? 'I knew a Mormon once,' I told them. 'He was one Honest Abe and he helped me through a tough time. I've never forgotten him or the things he told me.'

"Some people just get through to you, and you got through to me, hombre. And hey, you don't see guys in dress clothes on bikes much. I told the missionaries that I wasn't actually your religious type—that I wasn't even your serious type—that I was a comedic actress. They said there was plenty of room for humor in your church. I told them I believed them because I had a pretty funny friend once. Then I told them that he and the seriously religious friend were one and the same. YOU! Anyway, I've got an appointment this Friday morning for what they call a lesson with some women missionaries they're assigning to me. Don't get excited— I'm pretty sure nothing will come of it. But I still thought you'd get a kick out of it. I mean, can you think of a bigger joke? Me taking lessons in Mormonism? As if I'd ever qualify."

I read the letter three times, rushed to get a piece of paper, scrambled to find a pen, then hurried instead to the computer downstairs, hoping I could locate Allyson's old e-mails. After a good hour of trying to find her address, I finally shot off a note to her saying that her taking lessons wasn't funny at all, but fantastic. Then I gathered pamphlets and information and sent her a fat envelope along with the same message. I was glad I sent the backup, because the e-mail didn't go through. Alysse had apparently changed either her address or her provider, the way I had. A few days later I sent her even more information. Then I wondered if I'd overdone it because I didn't hear from her again, even after I sent a third sorry-I-overdid-it letter.

"If anything happens to come for me from New York, forward

it straight to my area," I instructed my mother as I got ready to head to San Diego. I was upset with myself for not sending Alysse my e-mail address in the previous letter. Why hadn't I done that?

It wasn't easy to readjust for the second time to missionary life. California wasn't Brazil and never would be. Even though I finally felt a confirmation that this was the place I needed to be, I still missed Brazil. Okay, San Diego's weather certainly wasn't anything to complain about, and the members were great to us and even gave us referrals. One afternoon my companion and I ran into a family from Portugal, and I had a chance to ask the golden questions in Portuguese. They wanted to know more! By concentrating on the work and praying, I adjusted. In fact, my companion, Elder Bonne, a native Parisian, and I began having some good success. In only a matter of weeks, however, I got a call from President Jackson assigning me to the office, where I was to perform the same duties President Phillips had had me doing in Brazil. It seemed I was destined to work with finances. Well, what can you do? When that's what the Lord wants from you, that's what you do.

By the end of my second month in San Diego, I was reorganizing and updating and getting things set up on the computer. One afternoon President Jackson had me come into his office. "I just wanted you to know, Elder," he said, "how nice it is to work with a self-starter who just goes ahead and gets the job done. If I'm giving you too much, will you let me know?" What could I do after he told me that? I worked even harder. In fact, in the evenings my new companion, Elder Sturgess, and I proselyted, and the time went by extremely fast. Because I was so busy, I didn't have much time to think about anything but missionary work. But every once in a while, when I passed a high school or a park, I found myself wondering what ever happened with my old friend Allyson Pringle.

Chapter Twenty-Nine

I'd been home from my mission several weeks and had been attending winter semester at Michigan State, saving up to go to school in Utah. One day, Mom called, catching me when I had run to my apartment to get some props and lunch. I had an hour or two between my Economics midterm and my presentation from *Barefoot in the Park* for my Basic Acting class. Yeah, even though I was going into accounting, I'd decided to take some acting classes just to add a little interest and balance to my life.

I had the phone handy and pulled it out of my bag as soon as I heard it ring. Monica had been complaining of pains recently and I wanted to make sure she was all right. It was a little early for her twins to be born, and we were all nervous that they might come before they weighed enough. Rulon was doing an internship with Ford and they were staying with Mom and Dad for a few weeks—at least until after the babies were born—so Mom could help. "Monica's fine," Mom said as soon as I answered. "The pains went away and no twins yet. I also called to let you know that you got three letters this week. Sorry I didn't tell you earlier, but with everything going on here, I just forgot. I can forward them to you if you want."

"Who wrote?" I asked.

"It looks like you got your regular postcard from Arnold, and then there's something from Elder Bonne in California, and then something else from an Hermana Adep, or something like that, from Ecuador. At least I think it says *Adep*. It's hard to read."

"Okay." I wasn't sure who I'd be hearing from in Ecuador, but I let Mom know I planned to come home over the weekend just to see if I could sleep for a change. My roommates enjoyed staying up until three or four each morning.

For the next two days, in between tests, I wondered off and on who would be sending me something from the continent south of us and who this Hermana Adep could be. I'd met a girl at a big interstake dance not long after I got home who was going on a mission, but it was somewhere in Europe. I was so curious by the time I got home that as soon as I'd done some serious hugging and had swung around the little tykes who were visiting and greeted old Lucky Duck, I headed for the mail basket.

Arnold's card was upbeat: a picture of a kangaroo and the corny caption: "Hoppin' you're having a good day." He said he felt sorry for me that I was home already from my mission, that he'd asked for an extension because he just couldn't face leaving his "favorite place in the whole world." He and his companion were teaching fourteen people, including someone who operated some kind of a kangaroo farm.

The card from Elder Bonne gave me the good news that the Pirone family had finally been baptized—all six of them. Yes!

I saved the mystery envelope for last. I couldn't really figure out the name: something like Adepp, just like Mom had said, but with two *p*s. Well, if it was from Allyson, it had to be a joke. Hermana, huh? Then it occurred to me that the letters in the name could be her initials. They *were* capitalized, and she'd always claimed to have a lot of middle names: Delilah, Eleanor, Penelope . . . In a hurry now, I reached for the letter opener, sliced it through the envelope anxiously, then pulled out the letter.

"Hello, Mr. Honest Abe," it started out. "Look what you started!" I coughed out a laugh. "Sorry I never answered your letters, but I was super busy repenting. If you thought I fell off the end of the earth, you're not the only one. In a way, I did." I eagerly reread those first few lines, my heart pounding, my hand shaking as I reached for a chair. "Last year I sent a card announcing my baptism to an address somebody gave me for you in Brazil," I continued reading. "But then I got it back, would you believe, six months later. I moved a couple of times after I wrote you, and I never could find your e-mail address. Well, anyway, here I am on a mission in Ecuador. Yes, you read that correctly!"

Okay, now I was sure this was a joke. It was all a joke. But there was more. "Like I told you in my first letter," she continued, "I met some missionaries in New York, and I ended up taking lessons. I'm sorry to say I was a little concerned about it for a while and I didn't make the progress I should have at first. That's why I didn't let anyone know and I didn't even tell you for a while. I should say I *thought* I told you about my baptism until the card came back.

After that I didn't write again because I was still a little afraid I wouldn't be able to be a good member of the LDS Church and that it wouldn't *take*. Okay, I'm being honest with you. You have to admit it's not your piece-of-cake (or *torta*) church.

"But then it did take. It really took—the Word of Wisdom, the whole thing. I found out I could get help if I'd just start relying on the gift I'd been given: the spirit of truth. And just like a former homeless guy in my last ward used to say, 'God's large and in charge.' It's so true. I finally let go and allowed myself to lean on the Big Guy and I just kept listening and living according to the LDS rules day after day. Pretty soon I found myself making progress. So I'm not keeping it a secret anymore. In fact, just a few months ago I had to decide between Broadway and a mission. Ha, like Broadway wanted me! Actually, I had started getting bit parts, but by that time I was a little disillusioned at the quality of the comedy. Too often I found myself reading lines that were in bad taste or raunchy. I'm not sure why people think garbage is funny. Then, get this, I turned down a final audition for Billie Dawn because, well, you should have seen what they wanted me to wear. Anyway, I put in my papers, as they say, and then I got a call to serve in Ecuador, and here I am.

"Kendall-Wendall, I gotta tell you that I feel like this is the best 'part' I've ever played—only I'm not playing a role. And who'd have guessed I'd someday actually be using the Spanish we learned in Alvarez's, huh? So, anyway, thank you for all you did for me but most of all for getting me interested in the gospel of Jesus Christ, mostly by just being who you are. You saved my life—literally, pardner. Have a happy day!"

I folded the letter, then unfolded it again. I checked the stamp on the envelope, still wondering if this was bogus. This was Allyson Pringle, after all. Was she really on a mission? I read the letter again, then again. No, I decided, this wasn't a joke. There was no way it was a joke. This was real!

At last, after reading the letter the third time, I was slipping it back into the envelope when I noticed a P.S. on the back of the last page that I'd totally missed before. I eagerly unfolded the letter again, turned it over, and read: "Since you had a lot to do with starting me down this road, or should I say *up* this road, I'm hoping you'll let me write you or e-mail you every once in a while with updates. I'd also like to get updates from you on how your life is going. Yeah, dating is definitely against the rules, but as far as I know *updating* is fine." I chuckled, then pulled the letter closer because there were a few lines that had been swirled through. I wasn't sure how honorable it was to try to read something somebody had tried to cross out, but something told me it was okay, and I studied those two lines carefully. Some words I couldn't make out at all, but I could read enough that I could tell it said something about her having written me many letters that she'd thrown away. I lifted it up to the light and read the words *scooped up* as well and realized she was telling me that if I wasn't "scooped up" before she got home, she would tell me more. Then I figured out that the last part read: *more in a position to do this.*

By the time I got the rest of the P.S. figured out, I was grinning so widely that it was a miracle my mouth didn't split in two.

"You okay?" Monica asked. I still wasn't used to my tall, skinny sister looking like she had a bed pillow tucked under her shirt.

"I'm *so* okay, Sis," I told her. "I'm so okay you wouldn't believe it. I just got a letter from Allyson Pringle—Alysse, an old high school friend. It's Hermana Pringle now. She was baptized and she's on a mission in Ecuador!"

"Are you talking about that girl you went to a dance with—the real character?"

"Oh, yeah," I said. "And she's definitely a character. But there's way more to her than that. Way more." I could tell that Monica wanted to know everything—all the details. Sisters are like that. But I honestly didn't know where to begin.

"Don't worry, I have the feeling you'll be meeting her some-day," I heard myself say. "In fact, I have this really strong feeling you'll be seeing quite a bit of Alysse Pringle."

"No joke?" said my sister, her eyebrows lifted.

I smiled and moved my own eyebrows up and down several times in a row. "No joke!"

About the Author

Born in the Netherlands, Anya Bateman came to Salt Lake City as a child and discovered early how much she enjoyed language, words, and writing. She attended both Brigham Young University and the University of Utah, graduating from the latter with an English degree and a creative writing emphasis.

Anya's stories and articles have appeared in the Church magazines as well as national magazines such as *Reader's Digest*. She is the author of several books for youth, including, most recently, *The Makeover of James Orville Wickenbee*. Looking back on things now, she feels grateful for her difficult and awkward teen years, as they have given her plenty of fodder for her writing.

Anya served a mission to California for The Church of Jesus Christ of Latter-day Saints, and she has served in several auxiliary leadership positions in the Church. She and her husband, Vaun, are the parents of four children and grandparents of seven.